Lauren's high school stands on the corners of Watergate and Post streets. Thus the name of her school newspaper, The Watergate Post. Compelled to write the story of her doomed newspaper, Lauren, a recent graduate, tells the story of its demise.

Running a high school newspaper can be a daunting task, especially when students have to work with outdated equipment, reluctant advertisers, and a difficult school principal. High school English teacher, eccentric and affable Bill Dombrowski, starts the paper, manned by a class of both under- and over-achievers. These students never expected they'd be so enthusiastic and dedicated. Even when some of the subject matter incurs the wrath of principal Silvers, the students prevail. But things change rapidly.

As the result of a silly editorial about the foul-tasting water in the school's fountains, Lauren and the other students come across a possible scandal, and the chase is on to gather evidence of a monstrous scheme to bilk the town residents out of their cash. They encounter political roadblock after roadblock in their search for the truth. Despite setbacks, the students are successful in blowing the whistle on the scheme. However, they are unprepared for the negative and downright vicious reaction from both the town fathers and the evildoers. Lauren and the entire high school unite to try and save their community and their teacher's job. The story is funny, sad and uplifting at the same time.

THE
WATERGATE
POST

Bruce Loper

A Black Opal Books Publication

Black Opal Books

BECAUSE SOME STORIES JUST HAVE TO BE TOLD

GENRE: COMING OF AGE/YA

THE WATERGATE POST
Copyright © 2021 by Bruce Loper
Cover Design by Transformational Concepts
Cover photos used with permission
All cover art copyright ©2021
All Rights Reserved
Print ISBN: 9781953434135

First Publication: FEBRUARY 2021

Published by Black Opal Books **http://www.blackopalbooks.com**

DEDICATION

"The Good Teachers"
the ones who love their students above all
the politics of the institution.

PROLOGUE

Everybody has a reason for writing a book: money, fame, ego, some stupid theme or moral—thanks Ms. Neihardt—a place to hide a bunch of symbolism that nobody except Ms. Neihardt can find or even care about, a chance to change the world—yes, I actually read *The Jungle* or most of it so you can't take away last year's diploma.—I am motivated by a simpler emotion: *REVENGE.* Maybe not in a Shakespearean sense, but I want this town to know what really happened in our school, what they did to Mr. D: what they did to us.

Of course, they changed all the names. They being the lawyers who work for the editors. Good guys, bad guys, businesses, everyone except me, changed. So, it may look like fiction. But it's not. There's a clue here and there, and symbols the air-breathers in the back row could find. So, if you really want to figure it all out, my name is still real and you can look me up and see where I'm from, what school I went to, and then with a little deduction, who all the idiots were.

This is dedicated to Mr. Dombrowski who made the mistake of caring too much in trying to teach us.

And everything in this book is true.

Lauren

CHAPTER 1
THE HIRING

Bryan was the first to see Mr. D., so I'll start at the beginning. Bryan was the new kid. He came from West Virginia and moved here just before school started. It took a long time to know Bryan, not because he was shy, but I think he and his dad moved around a lot after his mom died and he wasn't real out-going. Like me. That's a joke but you wouldn't know it yet. Bryan was in the office trying to register about a week before school started, but our old secretary didn't want to help him. She's the type who never wants to help anyone, though that's her job.

She told his dad, "You should have picked up a transcript from Welch before you left." That's probably about 800 miles from here. Notice that is a subtle clue. His dad probably felt like crap since he should have known, having moved so many times. I had to add that because I like using the word crap since that is a bad word here. Crap. Crap. Crap.

The old lady told Bryan's dad, "Welch will have to fax over a transcript.

"I doubt that Welch or all of West Virginia has a fax," he said.

She said, "Sit and wait."

So they did. Bryan figured they sat there for half an hour without the secretary moving and his dad didn't move. Finally Mr. Dombrowski came in.

The old witch said, "May I help You?" which is what she always said but never meant.

When you got to know Bryan better and Mr. D., which is what Bryan always called Dombrowski, Bryan acted out the secretary scene but not when Mr. D. was around. I'm sure he never saw it, and I'm sure Bryan exaggerated.

"I'm Bill Dombrowski and I have a 2 o'clock interview."

He wore a suit and he didn't look comfortable. It was tight in places like his mom bought it for him when he went off to college, and it was kind of wrinkled or slept in. But Bryan noticed right away Mr. D. was wearing black Nikes. The secretary seemed to see them, too, and she talked more to his feet.

"I'll see if he's ready for you." Her lips never moved. Over the next year I saw her do that many times and when we gave her the petition that comes later she said something like, "Thank you reprobates," though I know even she wouldn't call us reprobates, but it sounded like that so everyone all talked like that for a week without moving our lips saying, "Thank you reprobates." But we were still cool then.

Mr. D. sat down between Bryan and his dad because there were only three chairs and Bryan sure wasn't going to sit next to his dad. Mr. D. had some papers, which were for Mr. Silvers, the principal, the bastard, the antagonist, and Mr. D. set those on the floor. He pulled out these wads of Kleenexes from his pockets and was trying to wipe off his hands. They were dirty; I mean really dirty and not much of it was coming off.

"I got a flat tire not five miles from here," he said to

Bryan. I guess because he could see that Bryan was watching him. "That's why I'm late."

Bryan looked up at the clock above and figured the school mascot was some kind of a beaver but later learned was a wolverine, and saw that it was a good twenty after four.

"Spit on them," he said just trying to help, and Bryan always faked doing it.

Mr. D. just did this stifled laugh thing and Bryan figured he would sweat the dirt off soon enough. Just then the secretary came back in and told him to follow her, so he stood up. He tried to stuff all those Kleenexes in his suit pocket, but the pocket was a fake so he kind of had a handful of Kleenexes which struck Bryan as funny. He laughed, which made her look at him as Dombrowski bent to pick up his papers. When Mr. D. followed the secretary whose real name was Mrs. Budd and we called her Mrs. Butt for obvious reasons, Bryan looked under his chair and there they were so he picked them up.

His dad saw him and said, "He doesn't have a chance."

So, they sat there for a long time with Mrs. Butt just separating money, facing them all the same, squaring them all in neat little piles and counting them over and over stopping only to stare at Bryan and his dad now and then as if they were going to steal those stacks. She answered the phone when it rang and still didn't sound as if she really wanted to help anybody. Eventually Bryan got out his cell and started playing Tetris. His dad kept reading these little pamphlets and annoying him by saying things like: "They have a soccer team here. Maybe you'll want to try that. You were always fast." Or, "Look at all these science classes."

Bry looked but didn't want to. I guess his dad was

just trying to be nice on account of his mom leaving and that sucky school in Ohio where Bryan said you couldn't make a friend if you didn't play football. But the whole thing annoyed him anyway.

I have to change something here. I forgot something. That's the way that Bryan always told it, but Daryl (Colbert) corrected him one time and said, "You ain't got a cell phone." Daryl is really smart so he usually tries to sound dumb and says things like "ain't got."

He's right though. It was really a calculator, but Bryan didn't want to sound like one of those math geeks who write programs on their TI 83's and have LAN parties every weekend. It is good that I fixed it because I want you to know that everything in this is true except the names, but Daryl did call himself Colbert, but he pronounced it "kol-bert" as in Bert and Ernie.

No way Bryan could afford a cell phone. The last two places his dad worked just about went under, and he said Gorman's would fold and move production to China within the year. That's where he used to work. They made portable picnic tables, and I thought it was kind of funny when he said they would fold within the year because they fold up and stuff. He never found that funny, and now his dad's supposed to do quality control on boats for some job he found on the Internet. Bryan said his dad knew nothing about boats and never even owned one.

His dad continued to annoy him, and he continued to ignore him acting real interested in the Tetris and all. A fax came in but Bryan guessed it wasn't for them, because Mrs. Butt just looked at it and put it in one of those manila folders and sat back down to recount her money. You have to wonder if schools find secretaries who hate people or if the schools make them that way, although our Middle School had Ms. Zanco and she was great. In fact, I think she was the only person in that whole school who cared about kids.

Out popped Mr. D. with Mr. Silvers.

"Mrs. Budd will get you your books, have you fill out some papers and show you your room. This Friday will be staff day and kids will be here Monday. You ready for this?" So that's how Mr. D. got the job.

"I'm ready and excited. Thank you."

Mr. D. was still sweating even though by then it was kind of cold and Mrs. Butt had a sweater over her shoulders. "I'll start looking for an apartment this afternoon." He reached out his hand to shake Silvers' hand, but Silvers was telling Mrs. Butt to get him the books and show him his room, so he missed the handshake. Mr. D. kind of just used the hand to pull back his sleeve and look at his watch.

Mrs. Butt handed him the books, which were sitting right there on her desk and told him to run them out to his car and followed Mr. Silvers to his office all in one quick blur. Mr. D. left but Bryan heard every word she said.

"You can't hire this guy. He was late."

You could tell she didn't care if Bryan and his dad heard, but Silvers gave kind of a hard whisper.

"Look, he seems all right. He went to State and his grades are okay and the letter of recommendation from his mentor teacher was really good."

"At least check his references. If that is his best suit he's in trouble. And did you see those shoes? You've got to tell him he cannot wear shoes like that here."

"Look, I think he'll be okay. Plus, what choice do we have? School starts on Monday and I need a teacher."

"What about the blue-suit-lady this morning?"

"You didn't like her either."

"She was better than this."

"We would have had to pay her four steps on the scale and this guy is ground zero. He'll be okay, plus I told him maybe I could get him junior class adviser and parking lot duty for extra pay, and he seemed grateful. Can you imagine that?"

"There's no way this guy can do the prom."

"Give him a chance, besides, I already told him he has the job."

"Well, he can't teach here dressed like that. At least talk to him about the shoes."

She was back at her desk stacking money and looking as if she had said nothing when Mr. D. came back in. She handed him papers and a key and told him to follow her when another fax came in.

"He still doesn't have a chance," is all Bryan's dad said.

When Mrs. Butt came back, Mr. D. wasn't with her, so Bryan guessed he was either gone or down in his room. He looked at the fax machine willing her to check it, but she sat down to recount her money and neatly put rubber bands around the bills. So they sat. He looked at his dad and nodded at the fax machine, but his dad's not exactly the gutsiest dad in the world, so he didn't say anything to her.

Bryan cleared his throat and she gave him a look and he moved his eyes from her to the fax machine, but she chose not to follow. So finally Bryan said "Ma'am," and it's not like he's overly polite or anything, but it just seemed like his last chance to ever get out of there. "A fax came in while you were out."

She finished the stack she was working on and anyone could see she didn't want to get up but she did, and she walked all the way to the machine which was two steps and picked up the papers.

Bryan decided she was one-hundred and four. She looked the papers over, put them in a manila folder and sat back down. She was crushing that chair. Bryan figured by then Welch was closed, and they probably never got the fax request because they didn't have one and the request was just running around in little phone lines going brrrrrri-i-i-g-g-t-t-t-t looking for a home or a phone, which when she said, "Everything's in order. We'll have a schedule for you on Monday, the first day of school." Even his dad sighed when they left the office.

Then they both saw Mr. D. down by the drinking fountain. He was obviously trying to wipe something off the paperwork Mrs. Butt had given him. He didn't really look like the guy Mr. Silvers would someday call a danger to all us kids.

CHAPTER 2
DAY ONE

O n the first day of school all I could think was at least Kristin was in this stupid class. I was cool that we were going to have a newspaper, but I didn't want to write it. And this teacher guy was way too excited.

Kristin gave him a seven. Kristen is a nine-an-a-half. The only flaw I can see is kind of a bump in her nose where it turns down. I used to think she was loose and wouldn't care if she knew I wrote this. She's been with a lot of guys. Not for money or anything, but the way she explains it is guys have done it as often as possible for centuries and that was good, so now it was her turn, all women's turn. Take one for the women.

I don't follow her philosophy. We weren't there for two minutes and she had rated all eight guys not counting the teacher who she wouldn't touch. She always said teachers were off limits, and I think she kept to that, but she was with this guy last summer who was a lot older than this teacher. This teacher was Mr. Dombrowski. She, Kristin, picked out Kev for me and told me to watch his butt. I watched his butt. I'm not like Kristin, but I do think about sex all the time. Sex and food.

So Mr. Dombrowski was telling his life story, which

was like no life at all. School, school, two years of stupid jobs finding himself, school, school, and now here.
Who wants to be here? Kristin was saying Kev and I
can learn together, get how-to books because she thinks
I am smart because I read a lot.

Dombrowski asked us to say something about ourselves and called on Kristen because she was talking.
Teachers do that so it works for me that I almost never
talk.

Kristen looked him up and down and then up again.
"I plan on conquering the whole world."

And Mr. Dombrowski answered, "Oh good. Like
Napoleon, Genghis Khan, Alexander the Great?"

"I don't know about them. I'm going to do it one
man at a time."

"What's your name?"

"Kristin."

"Kristin, have you ever had a basic math class?"

"Two plus two of them Mr.—What is your name
again?"

"Dombrowski." I sucked in air. I knew she knew his
name. Half the teachers in the building would have sent
her to the office by now. "So Kristin…"

"Yes." You could tell now she was having fun.

"What brought you here?" He used a sweeping motion with his hand to take in the whole room.

"Well, I live on Maple, which is about three and a
half miles from here. I've got this job after school at
Subway downtown. My mom had to leave work early
and then rush back to finish her shift so she bought me
a car that I call Abigail after my grandma whose name
was Sadie.

"So I get in that car every morning and drive it to the
parking lot, which should have reserved spaces for up-
per-classmen, hustle my little butt in these size seven

shoes through these over-crowded halls and here I am," she added, while making a sweeping motion with her hand to take in the whole room.

Mr. Dombrowski was laughing. "We, and I mean that in the really big sense including all the possessives, are grateful you are here. And if you ever feel the need for a drama class, see your counselor."

I was glad to see he had a sense of humor.

"But back to the newspaper. We'll wait on the rest of you. Our goal, no, our mandate is to put out a news-paper every four weeks. We have six for the first one because this school has never put one out before, and as you can see, the only computer in this room is mine and that is used for grades and attendance. Mr. Silvers will be getting us six new ones within the week. In the meantime, all we have to learn is everything."

That became his mantra. "All we have to learn is everything."

He admitted to us, "I have never taught a newspaper class in my life, high school or college, but that will make this a little harder. I spent the whole weekend reading everything I could find about newspapers as well as looking for a place to live. Until I find a place, I will be driving almost forty miles each way.

"Anyone know of an apartment or small house to rent, cheap? Cheap is the keyword here. Do you guys have some sort of a slum here in town? Beyond the rail-road tracks? In the woods? Surrounded by an EPA su-perfund site?"

No answers. "Some place where I have to sleep with my nine-millimeter Glock under my pillow?" Still no answer. He didn't look like a guy with a gun. "Extra credit?"

There was a stirring. A couple of hands raised in-cluding Mollie's who he called on. She would die for one extra credit point. She was supposed to be smart and was going to be the valedictorian, but I sure didn't see it. The smart that is. She just did whatever the teachers told her to do no matter how stupid. Being a valedictorian is easy.

"I'll ask my dad," Mollie said. "He owns houses all over town." She gave him one of her little 'go ahead walk on me, I love it, smiles' and he smiled back falling for it completely.

"Actually, I should tell all of you, I don't believe in extra credit. All my assignments will be fair and my grading will be fair so you will all have the same opportunity to receive the grade you earn."

Then he turned back to Mollie. "However, if you find me a barn with heat, I will be eternally grateful and if your grade falls evenly between say a D+ and a C- I will probably most assuredly give you the C-."

Kristin snickered. She hated Mollie. I thought it was funny and I guess Mr. Dombrowski meant it to be funny, but Mollie was shaken. I don't know if it was the no extra credit or the thought of a C- but she was going catatonic. By the next day she was gone, having dropped the class, and she was replaced by an annoying girl from North Carolina who was all excited about everything and turned out to be all right.

As soon as Mr. D asked about housing, I thought of my Grandma's house, which was in the alley by our backyard. My dad fixed up part of the carriage house. She died the second week of summer vacation, less than a year after she moved in. I found her. She was white, white-blue. They said she stroked out, but I think she just missed Grandpa who died last year. She didn't do much of anything. I read to her a lot because her eyes weren't great with the diabetes. She played the television real loud, but I don't think she could hardly see it.

I missed her and sure didn't want a teacher with a gun, or without a gun, living there. It was Grandma's. So I didn't say a word. That's my policy.

So, Mr. Dombrowski talked about grades and attendance and I didn't really care about either. My parents always made me go and they didn't care what my grade was as long as I, "did my best."

They had stopped asking a long time ago if that grade was my best. Usually it was, but when I got an idiot like Mr. Dozier for U.S. History what did he know? We spent most of our time doing handouts of fill-in-the-blanks while he talked to the other coaches on the phone. I think the handouts were from the previous teacher whom my mom had. Regardless, we only made it to the Vietnam War and a lot sure has happened since then. That was a D+ and considering the quality of the teaching, it may have been my best.

Then Mr. Dombrowski talked about teamwork saying we were going to have to be a team if we were going to get the paper out.

"Everyone will be responsible to learn every job, and you will all switch assignments with each paper."

Kristin whispered she didn't like the looks of our team, although Jake could quarterback for her any time he wanted to. I pictured her bent over with Jake's hands on her butt as she hiked him story after story. My mind is somewhat warped sometimes, but I like it. Mr. Dombrowski saw her whispering, but then you could tell he thought better about calling on her.

He ambled over our way and stood near us. Another teacher trick.

"We will need reporters, photographers, a managing editor, editors, salespeople…did I tell you our paper has to be self-supporting? We have to raise enough money with each issue to pay for the printing and I have no idea what that will cost, but I will find out. I guess we will need permission slips so that you can drive around and sell ads."

Wow, that stirred up some murmurs. Driving around town on school time. Donut runs. Not that I needed donuts. The beach was an embarrassment with all these girls falling out of their suits in all the right places and me trying to pack it all in, in the wrong places. I almost never went to the beach, and when Gwennie called I often said I had to stay with Grandma, which really wasn't true, and Grandma was dead two weeks into the summer.

And it rained. It rained when they carried her out. It rained when the relatives came for visitation and they stamped their feet and shook off their umbrellas and then just hung around waiting for it to let up before they left, so we had all run out of things to say. How many times can I look sad and say, "I will really miss her?" Even though I will, you just can't keep saying it.

That's pretty much what happened the first day. I'm sure Mr. D said a lot more but I wasn't totally listening with my grandma and Kristin and all. He was still talking when the bell rung and he looked all confused.

"I guess that's that," he said. "I'll see you tomorrow." Half the class was practically out the door

CHAPTER 3
SLUTTY PRESIDENTS

You've got to understand Daryl. He liked Dombrowski right away from the second day. You could tell. Daryl walked in wearing a little clip-on Sunday black bow-tie and announced his new name was Colbert. It took the rest of us about two days to figure he was talking about Steven Colbert, and his sudden pronouncements such as, "I can see Wisconsin from my living room window and on a good clear day, Minnesota." which I knew was a reference to Sarah Palin, but most of the class thought him odd.

Maybe half the class liked him because you just had to know too much stuff to get him. It never bothered Mr. D. when he walked in the room after Spring Break and Colbert was mimicking him marching back and forth with his arms flailing saying we need to sell more ads and damn all Democrats. Mr. D. made him finish and then laughed as hard as anyone else in the room.

Dombrowski started that second day by asking, "Who are our best presidents?"

He did that a lot. You never knew where his questions were going to take us or what he intended. Once he started a class blindfolded and another time he was playing a guitar and singing a song, and he couldn't do either of them well. Actually, the song was in my

English class. I had him fifth hour. But another time he did the whole class only allowing those who never spoke to speak. No, that was English too, but I'm not going to take it out cause that was just how he was.

Kristin answered his president question with Kennedy of course, and Wayne threw in Bush and Reagan. Colbert asked, "Younger or elder?" and Wayne said it really didn't matter. And Colbert said, "There was a younger Reagan?" Wayne never figured out Colbert was making fun of him or that he wasn't a tea-partying, Limbaugh loving Republican.

"I don't know but if there was a younger, but I'd vote for him." I swear that Wayne listened to Rush on headphones during his lunch when everyone else had a life.

So Wayne asked Mr. Dombrowski what he thought of Bush and he asked, "Are you a millionaire?"

"No."

"Is your father, grandfather, or recently widowed Aunt a millionaire?"

"No."

"Well let me tell you then. I think Bill Clinton should have resigned. If he was a school teacher, or an insurance salesman, or for God's sake a clergyman who kept a stable economy, America basically at peace, an expanding middle-class, better opportunities for minorities, expanded environmental protections for everyone, and slept with an intern who wasn't a movie star or anything," he nodded to Kristin here since she had brought up Kennedy, "then lied about it in sworn testimony, that person would be deservedly fired."

"Undoubtedly, but I asked you about Bush."

"So, let me ask you. Did Bush keep a stable economy?"

"Yes. No. I guess not. But it really wasn't his fault."

"Damn right!" Colbert threw in. "But if he could

have gotten in just ten or more tax breaks for the wealthy, all us poor folk would be buried in money now."

"Keep America at peace?" Mr. D. asked glancing at Colbert like he shouldn't tease Wayne. It was his job.

"No, but he could have ended it if all the liberals had let him run it his way. Waterboarding's not torture, and even if it is, so what? Obama is even telling them ahead of time when he's going to pull out the army."

"We're talking about Bush now," Dombrowski said in that "easy boy, down" voice. "Did Bush expand the middle class or make better opportunities for the minorities, which would have to be the signs of a healthy country?"

Two slow no nods. For a moment I thought Mr. D. was getting to Wayne.

"Maintain progress in cleaning up our environment, the only one we have I might add?"

"No."

"Did he sleep with Monica Lewinsky?"

"Not that I know of."

"Then he did a fine job. Did I mention that I am rich? Filthy, stinking, pile-it-on rich? I get paid in less than two weeks and I'm already contracting with various armored car companies just to haul my first check out of here. Republican tax-breaks for the rich. I love them."

So maybe it was the third day Daryl became Colbert. Dombrowski couldn't have all the fun.

"So, who said Kennedy?" Mr. Dombrowski asked.

"I did," Kristin said. Every male head turned to her as they always did when she talked, and it was obvious it wasn't for her brains, though I think she was pretty smart inside. I leaned back because Kristen was right next to me.

"Why Kennedy?"

"Well, he did so many good things like civil rights, ask not and all that stuff."

"That 'ask not' speech was good, but I think you are mostly confusing him with LBJ. Kennedy was a slut and made Clinton look like a wimp." I'm sure no one in the room had heard a president called a slut before, especially a dead one. "He had great ideas but never got any of the legislation through Congress. LBJ passed Kennedy's legislation after he had Kennedy killed."

He left a dramatic pause waiting for the inevitable question. It came from Wayne. "You mean to say that Johnson killed Kennedy?"

"Sure. Why not?"

"But we learned John Wilkes Booth killed Kennedy." Erin said that. She was the new girl from North Carolina and talked with a syrupy southern accent. Colbert didn't care what she said and gave Kelly an evil eye when Kelly whispered "Moron" loud enough for everyone to hear. Erin was tall and competition for Kristin but not in a slutty way. One more person between me and a boyfriend.

"I'm sure they taught you Oswald killed Kennedy, but like everything else, they lied. Now," and he pointed at the whole class, "one thing I do not tolerate is criticism of each other. Leave the criticism to me. I'm packed with it. I get bonus checks every time I embarrass one of you. This class is going to be far too tough to beat up on each other."

"But Mr. Dombrowski. How do you know that Johnson killed Kennedy?" Wayne asked.

"I could have said 'I would have to kill you if I told you,' but that is getting old. You are just going to have to take my word for it or look it up yourself. It is just a commonly known fact with the intelligentsia of the world. And I am a part of the intelligentsia opening little doors into yours and everyone else's worlds to see if you want to join me. But not today. We need to get back to the good presidents."

"What about our first Republican president, Lincoln?" Wayne again.

"Lincoln was truly a great president, but he wouldn't fit very well in the Republican party today. Back then Republicans were liberal and about social change, trying to better the life of the downtrodden. Lincoln did a lot of good and lived up to his campaign promises. But the Emancipation Proclamation—that was an embarrassment."

"Why?" New kid, Bryan.

"Look it up. Don't they teach you anything around here?"

"I'm not from here," looking out the window like he saw a dog turd or something.

"This seems to me to be a good place to be from."

"It's okay so far," he admitted.

"It is for me too. But we need to get all the way to Jefferson."

"Why Jefferson?" Bryan again.

"Because this is a newspaper class." A long dramatic pause. Mr. Dombrowski did that often just to emphasize his points. We often had long dramatic pauses because we had no idea what he wanted. "What did Jefferson do before he became president?"

"He built Monticello," Bryan said. "I actually lived not too far from that once. Our class went there and it had automatic doors and a dumb waiter."

"And I'll bet it was there in the dumb waiter that he and Madison wrote the Amendments to the Constitution." Mr. Dombrowski rescued him. "That first one's a doozy. Anyone know it?"

This was when I noticed that everyone was paying

attention, even Sean who just never did. Erin guessed, "The freedom of speech which guaranteed a free press." She smiled that pretty southern smile that always made me question if it was genuine.

"That is a beautiful amendment, but I was asking you about 'doozy.'"

"Doozy?"

"Yeah. Weird word isn't it?"

"Weird." But I think she meant him.

"So, did you ever wonder where it came from?"

"No."

"Duisenberg cars. The finest cars in the world. Their advertisements said, 'That's a doozy' and it stuck with us. That's the problem with American English, every-thing sticks. How do I know all this?"

Colbert said, "Not how, but why."

"Why, because I was born fourth generation Ameri-can English with a bunch of mutts thrown in, so every-thing sticks, and how, because my great grandfather built Duisenbergs until he was laid off in the middle of the Great Depression. Now the cars are worth millions and my great grandfather died poor, still hating Roose-velt."

"But you're rich," Colbert said.

"Yes I am, and I still have the First Amendment which Miss...What is your name?"

"Erin."

"Which Miss Erin so eloquently stated. Erin, did you know we have a class here called English as a Second Language?" She blushed and grinned. Colbert was leaning out of his seat staring at her and Kristin didn't look too happy. School was her territory.

"Now Jefferson and Adams were like Wiley E. Coy-ote Super-genius' compared to about any president we've had since. Why do you suppose they put

'Congress shall make no law limiting the freedom of speech, or of the press' first?"

Nobody said anything.

"Come-on class. This class is about thinking. Guesses are cheap and not very painful. You over there avoiding eye contact at all costs, what's your name?"

"Sean."

"Sean, why did they put it first?"

"Because it was called the First Amendment so that seemed the appropriate place for it." I never knew Sean was that quick and about half the class laughed and the other half again looked at Mr. Dombrowski for his re-action.

"Good answer Sean. Now let's pretend they had let's say about ten amendments laying around and none of them had been numbered yet. Why did they put that one first?"

"They probably thought it was the most important."

"Very good. Excellent. Yes, it was the most im-portant then, and it remains the most important today. It's what separates us from the also-rans of the world. It's what makes this country a decent place to live. It's not Wal-Mart. It's not 214 channels of digital TV in-cluding re-runs of The Beverly Hillbillies. And it's sure not Banquet frozen apple pie. It's the First Amendment. I guess that leaves out Chevy Trucks too."

Once Mr. Dombrowski got started, you just couldn't stop him. He just rolled. Sure, he was opinionated. I should say super-opinionated, but he was right about just about everything. He made us think about every-thing we believed in. And sometimes I think he just said crap to get our reaction.

"You know, Jefferson set the government up with a series of checks and balances, but I believe he meant the press to check and balance all three branches of the government. The fourth pillar or fourth estate. He figured the government was just going to be filled with a bunch of self-serving politicians and somebody needed to watch over them."

"Obama," Wayne whispered loud enough for everyone to hear.

"Yeah," Colbert chimed in. "Here he is a poor Muslim from Africa getting rich in our system."

"Can we finish with Jefferson first?" Nods. "For the most part Jefferson was right. Someone needs to oversee the politicians. I don't think that many people go into politics as a method to get rich, but they sure come out that way. Anyone here read Wolfe's 'A Man in Full?'"

No hands.

"You need to. The average senator today is as rich as me and has to raise something like five thousand dollars every day he is in office just for reelection. Remember when your mom told you that you could grow up to become president? She lied. She probably lied a lot. Heck, Erin. She lied about you being cute. Anyone but a mother could see your left dimple is way bigger than your right dimple and that leaves your whole face lopsided."

Erin grinned and I doubted her face was lopsided. "I won't even go into some of the lies your mothers told the rest of you, but she did lie when she said you could become president. Presidential campaigns are now billion-dollar Madison Avenue farces, and I'll bet no one in here except me and any of you who become California movie stars can raise that kind of cash and hold on to your integrity."

Here he went into this acting thing with some rich guy wanting a certain vote and the politician wanting a certain amount of money but being unable to ask directly. It was funny with him playing both parts.

"Now, if you witnessed this conversation, could we print it in our paper?"

There was a general argument with the consensus being that it was okay but others arguing we would need another witness or a videotape.

After surveying the class he said, "Yes, we could publish it. You are a professional reporter acting in a professional manner. In fact, I think the First Amendment makes us duty-bound to do so. Witnesses would be great but not mandatory. Besides, what good did videotape do for Rodney King? Don't answer that. You probably don't even know who he was, but he was a poor black man who got beat almost to death by cops. Someone videotaped it and the cops were still found innocent. Well not innocent, but not guilty. We don't have time for that today. The second question is, would we?"

No argument there. We would put it on the first page, and I secretly wished it was me who heard the conversation. I could see myself being the youngest recipient of the Pulitzer Prize. Maybe I could then buy a senator and turn it into some real cash.

My mind was really going out there when he asked, "Do you know what hell your life would be if you printed that story? Threats of lawsuits. Actual lawsuits. Trips to the principal's office. Accusations of slander. Grounded for a week. FBI leaks to the press about the time you forged your mother's name on an absence excuse, and the fact that you sucked your thumb up 'til Kindergarten and then sometimes when you just needed the reassurance that only a good thumb can give. Still going to print it?"

Less enthusiasm now. A lot less.

"You have to. Obviously we would also have to be

very careful you had the facts straight, but we'd print it. That's what we are here for."

"Obviously we are not going to get this story despite the fact that bribery in the name of campaign contributions goes on 24/7. Let me take that back. Not the bribery thing, the 24/7. It's too clichéd for a quality class like ours. We are going to get some good stories, so we need to learn how to properly record them and write them. In other words, all we need to learn is everything about becoming good journalists.

"Since I don't know how to do that and we have no textbooks to teach us, I am going to show you a movie by the best journalists I know of, Woodward and Bernstein. Now it's an old movie and I apologize for that, but Robert Redford looks a lot like Brad Pitt, who looks a lot like me, and there must be something in it for you guys, too. I like it. Plus I borrowed a journalism textbook from a college buddy. It's my homework. So I will supplement as much as I can as soon as I get that baby read. It's about this thick."

He held out his hands about six inches apart. I could see one on his desk and it was maybe an inch and a half, but I always liked it when he exaggerated. "Oh the sacrifices I am willing to make for you. I was supposed to go out with Miley Cyrus tonight. It's going to break her heart when I tell her I am staying home, reading this book for you."

He just let us have the last three minutes or so to ourselves. You could tell he was pretty proud of his finish, leaving us wondering if he really was dating Miley. Of course we all knew that was probably just a name he picked up somewhere not realizing she just reentered rehab and not in this state.

CHAPTER 4
BRAD PITT

So we watched the movie, "All The President's Men." It was from a long time ago and was true about two reporters, Woodward and Bernstein, who took down Richard Nixon, who was supposed to be the worst president of all. It wasn't like when we screwed around in Spanish class watching "Finding Nemo," in English no less. Everybody watched this one and everybody believed in journalism and everybody wanted their piece of the First Amendment.

Kristen wanted a senator. Colbert wanted a Republican as he railed against Democrats. Wayne wanted to meet Deep Throat in a dark hall and hear him whisper, "Follow the birth certificate." I admit, I too wanted to expose corruption, maybe if only at this school.

Sean was the weird one. He was reading the book, too, and kept saying they left this or that part out, and the book was way more tense. I think he was far smarter than he looked and far smarter than his grades. He just needed to wash his hair more often and brush his teeth a lot more often. When Kristin told him once to wash his hair—she'll tell anybody anything—he asked her if she ever reads Calvin and Hobbes, "…the one where Calvin made his bed in a room full of clutter and chaos and his mother is praising him." Well that's me. I love it when I meet the minimum of someone's expectations.

"You're not even on the planet of minimum expectations yet," Kristen replied. But it didn't hurt his feelings. He once calmly told Dombrowski that he was the smartest person in the class, and that might even include Dombrowski who kept interrupting the movie to make a point such as, "Notice how they needed a second source for that fact," or "That was really just a rumor so they couldn't use it."

Sean corrected him once and said the movie shortened a particular scene, and it turned out one of the things they printed wasn't entirely true because they misquoted a source. Mr. D. was cool because he let Sean spell it all out to us. Most teachers would have shut him down, or at least most of the teachers here.

Mr. D was definitely cooler than most of the teachers—calling some of them teachers was a serious exaggeration—in this place. Some of them are so stupid or lazy, and then they have to listen to Mr. Silvers the principal, who is the stupidest one of all. And a hint for you, since most principals are probably just like Silvers. If you ever get sent to the office, all you have to do is give him a line of Dickens type crap and they fall for it every time.

If you are really jammed up, then say you are going to bring in your parents and your mom's a screamer, or your dad is a lawyer. No way they'll deal with a screamer, so they just send you back to class where the teacher will pass you just to get rid of you. Everybody knows this.

Not that I ever did much wrong. I told you that. I just do my "best" and ignore the really stupid ones. Bitely, who teaches American Government, just wanted us to copy her notes from the board and turn them in at the end of the week so she can check your handwriting--or

something. I did it but Sean refused and just asked her
current American Government questions, which she
couldn't answer, and she passed him. I'm sure so she'd
never have him in class again.

But my point about the movie is it really was our
downfall. We all wanted to be Woodward and Bernstein
and bring somebody down. Maybe that's why I'm writing this book, still wanting to bring someone down. To
be a journalist was to be a detective in a higher sense.
When Deep Throat said, "Follow the money," I realized
that's what it was all about. Money equals power,
equals politics. And ethics is not part of the equation.
But journalism can be the saving grace. And no matter
what Silvers and Superintendent Farroll said, Mr. Dombrowski taught us good journalistic techniques. All our
stories were accurate. They had to be or we wouldn't
print them.

CHAPTER 5
GET HIM WHILE HE'S CHEAP

So we were still learning about journalism when the computers arrived. Gawd they were controversial all year. Now I'm no computer genius, that was Matt who couldn't do anything else, but every time I turned one of those things on I just said a silent prayer hoping that I could do a complete layout or write my article without having everything disappear in a crash. They were XPs, circa 1999, towers, all of them.

Sometimes whole pages disappeared right at deadline, and we all had to stay after school and throw a page back together, but they were never as good and everyone couldn't show up. We screwed up an ad bad one time that way, but we ran free ads in the next two editions. Remember our paper had to be self-supporting so that cost us real money. And I think a lot of people who bought ads did so out of pity and never really expected to make their money back. But we did our best; we really did. You can imagine how those old computers made us feel.

We came to class on the second Wednesday and there were four computers sitting on the floor up front by Mr. Dombrowski. He didn't look as happy or excited as I thought he would.

I remember he said, "Well, our computers are here.

They're not exactly as promised, but the 'gurus that be' assure me that they will do."

"Gurus that be" of course turned out to be the computer techs who ran around the school. Matt knew more than all of them put together. Even I could see that four computers for sixteen people was about four too few and two less than Mr. Dombrowski expected. Of all the old XPs, not even one of them had a big flat-screen monitor, which is what we needed. We had to make do with balky fat CRTs, which, with their towers, took up a lot of room, which we also didn't have.

We all pitched in and cleared two tables in the back and carried the computers there. Mr. Dombrowski was trying to look like he knew what he was doing running wires from one computer to the next, but everyone could see he knew nothing. Someone suggested Matt. I didn't know Matt knew anything about computers let alone everything. He just kind of existed up to this point. He was the kind of guy your mother would want you to date, except he never dated anyone, probably because your mother would want you to. He wanted to. It became kind of a class joke, but Matt was right in the middle of it.

I think it was the week after homecoming and we were trying as a class to come up with an angle for a losing football season, when Matt raised his hand up right during the first ten minutes of class when we were supposed to be discussing problems and solving them.

"Mr. Dombrowski, do you think you could get me a date?"

"Huh?" I'm betting college never prepared him for that question.

"I need a date. I've never really had one and I think you could set a goal to get me a date by prom time."

"How am I to do this?"

"You can do anything Mr. Dombrowski."

"Just a date. Anyone in particular?"

"A girl."

"That's a good place to start. We have girls in here. Lots of them. Any of you girls want to go on a date with Matt?"

No answers. No one wanted to seem desperate.

"Extra credit?" Pause. "Okay. One date with Matt. No handholding. No good night kiss. You just have to be seen in public with Matt, maybe walking within an arm's length on the way to the movie theater." Pause. "It doesn't look good Matt. Are you maybe like a serial killer or something? An alien? You don't seem all that ugly to look at but what do I know? Come on girls. Five hundred extra credit points. Anyone?"

Kevin told Matt if Mollie was still in the class, she'd do it for five hundred points. Mr. Dombrowski gave Kevin a dirty look but turned away when it looked like he was going to laugh. The rest of us knew no one would ever see those points.

"Sorry Matt."

"Don't give up, Mr. Dombrowski. You are my best hope."

"That's kind of sad. I don't really understand women. I appreciate the fact they all fall in love with me, but I don't know why. Maybe I'll read some of my fan mail tonight and see if there are any clues. In the meantime, maybe we can come up with an advertising campaign."

Within a week, Mr. Dombrowski and Matt started their "Get Him While He's Cheap" campaign. Mr. Dombrowski figured that Matt was the next Bill Gates so there's no pre-nup with the first wife. If he became a billionaire, the first wife would get half. It really wasn't successful, but we had a lot of fun and even ran ads for

Matt whenever we had empty space to fill.

Everybody who answered signed other people's names. For the Christmas edition I came up with the slogan, "Meet Matt's evil side," and my friend Danni drew pictures of Matt stealing from kids' stockings, whipping Rudolph, and kicking an elf into a snowbank. Mr. Silvers hated them of course but Matt asked for the originals. Every girl likes a little bad boy.

But it was Matt who stunned the class that first day with the computers when he announced, "These computers will never run the software. There's room on the hard-drives, but not enough RAM and the processors are a joke. We need a server." Mr. Dombrowski wrote it all down and took it to the gurus and powers that be and nothing was ever done. See why we got so mad.

Matt was right. The computers were never stable. They crashed and crashed and often didn't run. If you waited for the "computer experts" we could go a week without a computer and miss our deadlines. Matt's sole job became keeping the computers running. He scammed parts from everywhere and I know he switched computers with Miss Bitely when she had a sub. She never used her computer. I think she just waited until the end of the semester and graded every student on how much she liked or disliked them.

I know this whole thing drove Mr. Dombrowski nuts. I know he went back to Mr. Silvers many times and several times he'd be excited the next day telling us that we had new computers on the way, or that Mr. Silvers went to Mr. Farrell, the superintendent, and Farrell would say, "They are looking for the money."

Farrell didn't look. The football team always had money. The parking lot got re-tarred. Neither computers nor upgrades ever arrived, and you could tell as the year progressed it took a toll on Mr. Dombrowski, but he never told us. He smiled when we lost pictures and always said help was on its way. But it was less genuine and more sarcastic as the year progressed.

After we watched "All the President's Men," we went on a class trip to the local newspaper and they taught us how they put their paper together. They had these great big fast computers and Matt was in heaven. They'd take a digital picture and crop it and adjust it and paste it right on the page. When the page was finished, which took maybe two minutes, they keyed it right over to the printer, articles and all. They gave us lots of short cuts, editing techniques, and advice. Matt could do it as soon as they showed us, and Kevin and Maggie were almost as good. They said if we had a server to put it together as a unit, we could attach the whole thing directly to their printer using our broadband. We were hyped.

Can't you see why we were so disappointed when Silvers got us those junk computers and then basically abandoned the class? Server? No. Broadband? No. How hard we worked to put out a decent paper only to see it crash and disappear on deadline day? Digital camera? What a joke. We used our phones but they had too many pixels for the program. Silvers too. Most of us had better computers at home. Pictures, ads, articles, and paste. That was us.

Maybe I should have taken Dombrowski up on the date with Matt thing. This was my senior year and I had decided to go to homecoming and it was going to be with Tim in my math class. What does it take with boys? I asked him for help on problems at least three times, and I think I understood them better than he did. I wanted to shake him and say, "Hey, this is me, Lauren. I don't talk and I don't need your help. Let's go to the dance." But I didn't. Why is it so easy for Kristen? He never asked and I ate a lot of pizza that night. I almost hate myself when I do that.

CHAPTER 6
CARAMELS AND SEX

K risten and I got a lot closer thanks to the news-paper; some good and some bad. I would never say we were best friends, because no one was ever best friends with Kristen, and I suppose that was true for me, at least since Grandma died.

Kristen told me things she didn't tell anyone else, although towards the end she talked to Dombrowski a lot and even told him about her father. He had written her from jail or when he was just released from jail tell-ing her he wanted back into her life. If she'd send him some money, he'd come visit. You need to understand she hadn't seen him since she was three and he left her mom. She sent him almost three hundred dollars and apparently that was all he wanted because he never showed up. She was hurt but didn't want it to show.

Kristen also told me about some of the guys she'd been with and that it was really about power. "You should just watch them, Lauren. I flirt with them a little and they get all stumble-mouth and weak in the knees. I'm in control. You should try it." She loved turning my face red.

"That's just not me," I'd say or something equally stupid sounding. "And my dad would kill me."

Hanging around Kristen made me kind of appreciate my own dad. It had been years since he knew what to say or do, but at least he was there and he tried. I'm not going into my mom. My mom had problems since Grandma died, and that meant she and my dad had problems, and they were doing a lousy job hiding it from me.

I was in my own thoughts when I heard, "At least you have onr parent at home who cares for you. The closest thing I ever had was an uncle who messed me up at nine and I had to testify against him at eleven. Try that," leaving me wondering what I missed.

But I don't want you to think of Kristen that way. Her stories changed all the time so you never really knew which ones were true. She just liked getting reactions from me the same as she liked reactions from the boys.

"I've read all that psychology crap and that's not why I've done what I do," Kristen said.

"Everyone does it except you and Matt and maybe Erin and I'm really not even sure about Dombrowski. But just about all the kids here do it. It's the same everywhere. It's only the parents in denial. No really. You want Kev, I'll get him for you."

"Thanks, but I'm handling it," I said.

"What you are handling is the caramels you hide in your purse and never share."

"That's mean. If you want a caramel, just ask."

"I'd like one, but don't think it's going to make me give up boys." She laughed.

Like I said, she reveled in shock, and she liked to hide it with her humor knowing there was always a little truth to her humor.

In some ways with her background she was shouting out, 'Hey look at me. I am Kristen, and I am somebody.'

Probably the opposite of what I did most of the time. 'Hey, don't look at me. I'm no one.'

Nobody cared more about the paper more than Kristen did. She didn't really like school, but somehow the paper gave her a voice and a byline and respect. And maybe that's what she needed most.

Kristen named the paper. We had a contest. Everyone had to come up with a name and we wrote them all on the board and had a vote. The others all made up school type names and one wanted to keep the name of the old paper from years before, which was just some little photocopy, obscene thing. It really was obscene. They swore in it and everything, which was kind of cool when they did music reviews, but the paper really was a joke. No one read it. We all had to read it to see what we weren't going to do.

Dombrowski wouldn't let us swear, ever. Since we had just finished "All the President's Men" and our school was on the corner of Gates and Waters Streets, Kristen suggested the WaterGate Post. It sounded classy, and we all wanted a classy newspaper. When we voted, it was unanimous. That lit her up.

We spent two or three days discussing what type of pages we would have in our first edition and what type of articles to write for each page. Since we were running out of time, we decided on just four pages, but they would be on real, full size newsprint and we would add pages as we gained experience. We had a student news page, an editorial page, an entertainment page and a sports page. I don't know what it is about guys and their sports. Every guy except Daryl—Oh, I'm sorry, Colbert—wanted to write sports stories. Well maybe not Sean. He didn't appear to really want to do anything.

So each page had to have its own editor and people to volunteer to write articles for it. Each editor had to write at least two stories and was ultimately responsible for what their page looked like. We had a managing editor, Kevin. My Kevin though obviously not mine. He was responsible for everything. The paper had to be on time, neat, appropriate, and pay for itself, which Dombrowski told us cost about $300 per issue. We had to print enough to give one to each student in the high school. I think Kevin volunteered for the first edition because he was the biggest guy in class, so he figured he was meant to rule. He did okay. Kristen was obnoxious elbowing me every-time he bent over some copy.

Somehow Kristen got chosen ad manager. She was whispering to me and the next thing I knew, there she was, ad manager on the board. Three hundred dollars to raise; she and three other students. And they still each, except Kristen, had to write an article for one of the pages. By the time all the jobs were assigned, it was obvious that sixteen people, one hour a day, and four weeks were not enough to put out a paper.

We filled two whole blackboards with ideas for articles, places we might sell ads to, pictures we might take, deadlines, and suggestions for how we might lay out the pages. It looked impossible. In fact, it was, since we were more than a week late with the first paper.

Mr. D. taught us that ads rule the paper. We developed our ad price by finding out how much the local paper charged per square inch and dividing that figure by fifteen since their circulation averaged fifteen times as much as ours was going to be.

We figured out exactly how many square inches of ads we had to run to produce three hundred dollars and then assigned one third of them to each of the three pages. We all agreed we didn't want ads on the front page. This actually controlled how much space we had for the nonexistent pictures and articles, which then went back to Kevin.

What I liked about Dombrowski was he trusted us to do our work. Kristen figured out the price and showed it to him, and he just said, "Great. Go sell the ads." This was for Kristen a new kind of power and she took right to it.

Dombrowski got us papers from other schools, some good, some not. So we used the good ones as examples. There are a lot of methods and choices in setting up a newspaper with fonts, and cut lines, and headlines, and type-sizes, and white-space. So Kevin, and anyone not doing anything except Matt, worked on that. Matt was still Mr. Computer Superhero, but that wasn't going well. Kristen and I read the whole yellow pages looking for likely targets, and we divided them into two teams, which set off each day selling ads, designing ads, proofing ads, or eating cookies.

The Cookie Lady was Carol, as in Carol's Cookies, and our first sale. She was a sweetheart. She made these giant cookies that probably had a thousand calories and every time we walked in, she gave us each a cookie. We found lots of reasons to come back. She agreed right away to buy a twenty-five dollar ad, but we had to show it to her before we could print it. We showed it to her, ate cookies and she'd make a little suggestion, and we'd fix it, and show it to her, eat cookies, and she'd make a little suggestion.

She really was a perfectionist. She had gone out of business before our last paper came out. Gawd, I loved those chocolate chip cookies with walnuts, especially when they were still warm and gooey. I'd buy two after she gave us one. But my point is, Carol was just a nice lady who saw we were doing a good thing and she tried to help us.

When we got back from Carol's or anyplace else, we

needed one of the four computers if all four were running. We often came in during lunch and after school, but we had to get our ads the way the customers wanted them. We drew them and imported graphics and got the font just right and bang, they were all over the place looking nothing like what you started with. We learned that the moment you got an ad right you printed a copy, assuming the printer was working. Later you could literally paste it onto the page.

When we printed the first paper, each full-size newspaper page was supposed to come out of the printer in six neat sheets. Then we were supposed to cut and paste them on the big sheets that Mr. Dombrowski delivered to the city newspaper to be printed. Good theory. Sure, they printed out, but not right.

They printed crooked, over and over. Even Matt couldn't make those stupid computers work right. Not enough RAM. The first two pages were always good and then it would start warping right. Halfway down the page we had to cut it line by line and paste them to the page.

The pictures or ads always had to be rerun. It was a joke. It was supposed to be so simple, but I'll bet it took us four hours to finish those first four pages. And this was after school. Maybe it was two hours, but it was so frustrating with people running around and every time I looked up that sleaze Sean was trying to look down some girl's shirt, so he'd quick look away. Did he think we were stupid? And why did he stay? It wasn't like he was really doing any work.

I'd love to see Silvers try to glue little strips of paper to a big sheet while holding his shirt closed with the other hand any time Sean was around. I'll bet that if he'd had to print a report or papers on whatever it is that he has to do and the system didn't work any better than ours, he'd have a new system there in four minutes flat.

This went on all year. Our printer never got any better, but we got a little faster as we learned new tricks. Of course, the papers kept getting bigger so it still took us a couple of hours after school each time. We all learned to wear sweatshirts.

We almost made the three hundred dollars for that first paper. Kristen and I sold two hundred seven dollars and fifty cents worth of ads. Randy and Anna only sold seventy-five dollars worth and fifty of that was to his dad who owned the framing shop downtown. Personally, I've never seen a kid buy a frame. The word was that Randy and Anna were going to the cemetery and making out when the weather was nice and parking at Wal-Mart when it wasn't. I'm pretty sure Dombrowski got wind of it too, but he never said anything to the class. Guys and girls were just never allowed to team up alone after them. It simply became, girl/girl, guy/guy, or threesomes. I think Dombrowski made up the seventeen-fifty we were short.

And it was about a week before the paper came out that he moved into Grandma's house. My parents ran an ad, and I begged them not to rent to him, but they never listen.

CHAPTER 7
FIRST EDITION

The first paper was great, but I learned Kevin was a jerk. He sweet talked all the girls and Mr. Dombrowski of course, but he embarrassed and humiliated the guys at every chance if he thought it made himself look a little better to the girls.

He used to come up behind Bryan, the new kid, and pretend to break off one of his arms and say he needed it to reach in the slot of his locker, or to get the keys out of his car 'cause there was no hanger available, or he used it to pattern a new backscratcher.

He did this right in front of Erin once after Bryan had finally gotten the nerve to talk to her about North Carolina. He told her about how he and his dad went to Wrightsville Beach and how terrific it was. I could tell he was nervous and had prepared way too long for this conversation.

Kevin saw it too, checked where Dombrowski was, and did the hanger thing. I know some girls fall for that crap, but I think it set Erin to liking Bryan. She "Wrightsville Beach" real loud so everyone including Dombrowski turned to look, and Kevin had to let go of Bryan's arm. Then they had a whole conversation about her being from the mountain side of the state. I stopped looking at Kevin's butt.

Kevin was really an artist at heart. I'll give him that much. He could just see how a page should look. He turned the "T" in The WaterGate Post into this giant walnut tree that ran down below the banner. He seemed to have a knack for getting the pictures the right size and the headlines concise and bold, not that we needed anything too bold in the first issue. To his credit, his was probably the best looking of all the papers, and the other managing editors all tried to get theirs to look like his. Of course it was our smallest issue at four pages and he didn't need to be such a jerk.

The sports page was pretty typical high school. Mr. D. had only one rule for the sports page: no dumb jock stories. He said you could find them in every paper in every town in America and the dumb jocks got fawned on enough.

He challenged us to find the stories no one else wrote about. Mr. D. seemed to have some kind of latent anger towards successful jocks. Maybe he dropped the ball in a big game and never played again, or he got his butt kicked by a star quarterback at a school dance. I shouldn't pick on him. He never really picked on me, but I'm guessing he wasn't much of an athlete. His arms were as skinny as Bryan's.

I think Bryan wrote the best sports story. It was about his friend Whitlow. He had the locker next to his, rode the same bus and it turned out, lived two houses down. Both his mom and his dad worked at the same boat plant as his dad, only Whitlow's dad sprayed glass. Everyone in town learned right away who the glass-sprayers were. They all had tape marks on their wrists, chins and ankles from taping their suits and gloves on. They were usually skinny too. I don't know if they were hired that way to fit in the boat or if they sweated down to that.

But Whitlow was a great bike rider. He and his father rode all the time and Whit started racing when he was twelve. He had to race against mostly older kids and still won most of the time. A British coach saw him in a Canadian century when he was sixteen and told his dad he needed to ride in Europe to see how good he could become.

I think his parents sacrificed a lot to send him there but he spent the whole summer racing all around Europe. No one expected him to win anything. He was lucky to break the top fifty in the first few races, but gradually his times improved and he started to place. Before he left for home, he had won two major events and no one except his family knew about it.

Whit is basically pretty shy, and Bryan had to get most of the story from his dad. Mr. D. thanked Bryan and said that was a perfect story—after Bryan rewrote it at least six times—and Whitlow became kind of a school hero, but it didn't go to his head. Whitlow wasn't in any of my classes so I never considered going to Homecoming with him. I wouldn't have an excuse to start a conversation.

Randy wrote an article on James Dawson, a senior, who spent four years on the bench for our football team, and remember, we had a lousy team. And James didn't care. By the time the article was written, he had never touched a ball in a game or played a single down. And he loved it. He even broke his collarbone in practice during his sophomore year and he didn't care. He said being a part of the team was the highlight of his school years and probably his life. It was a good article too.

The others were just okay, except for Jake's rah rah football team thing, but we all knew Jake had to write that and we had to print it. There was a neat picture of Ms. Oakley, the girl's basketball coach, who looked like she was praying for a victory, or the clock to run out, or maybe for the game to be over. We wrote a cut line about the separation of church and state and blew the picture up real big. She had her eyes closed and everything.

The best thing you could say about the entertainment section was that it was opinionated. We reviewed music, movies and video games and we told the kids exactly what we thought. If something was crap, we said crap. If it was cool, we said so. The "crap" thing kind of got us in trouble. Silvers got all bent because some mother's innocent daughter brought home a paper with the word crap in it, and she wanted to know if the school was condoning the word crap.

Now I don't know the girl, but Kristen said she was a sleaze and Kristen is the expert on that. So Mr. D., Kevin, and Amy who wrote the article had to meet with Silvers. They armed themselves with a copy of the old paper (which used actual swear words), a current issue of the *New York Times,* which used the word crap in a headline, and a Webster's Dictionary.

According to Kevin, who told Randy, who told me, Silvers never listened to anything they said. He just said we cannot use words like that because he never wanted to get another call from an irate parent over words used in the school paper. Randy said Kevin said you could tell that Mr. D. really had to hold it in. He kept asking Mr. Silvers what he liked about the paper, and all Mr. Silvers wanted to talk about was what he didn't like. So crap, crap, crap. Now I feel better.

The editorial page was nothing to get excited about. Well Colbert was excited. He ranted about Democrats saying that Republicans should get two votes each since it was a well known fact Republicans were twice as smart as Democrats. I'm betting most of the people who read that column didn't see the humor and just nodded and said, "so true."

He ranted about a Wal-Mart going up in town saying that it will finally close all the little shops downtown that clutter up the view. He never said what we were supposed to view. And he ranted about bumpy school busses without giving any solution at all. What that had to do with anything, I don't know. I'm guessing he was one of the few seniors riding a bus.

We ran some fake letters to the editors just to generate an interest and leave an address to write actual ones. Kristen was still on that upper-classman-reserved-parking-spot kick. She actually got a lot of support in future issues.

The front page may have been the start of all our future problems, but you couldn't see it then. It began with Mr. D. One day the first week, he came into class practically gagging. I should say that he was almost always a few minutes late, because he usually walked the parking lot during first hour conference giving out tickets and yelling at speeders.

The tickets were orange stickers that were about impossible to get off your window if it was hot but collectors' items if it was cold. Kids stuck them on their books, other kid's cars, and sometimes their lockers. The second sticker was supposed to be a tow, but Silvers never towed anyone, because that risked parents yelling at him.

I felt sorry for Mr. D. because all the kids knew that, so they parked wherever they wanted and collected stickers like baseball cards. So Mr. D. was gagging and asking the class if anyone ever drank the water from the drinking fountain in the English wing.

Erin replied, "They told me on my first day to never drink the water here."

"Anywhere?"

"Nowhere."

"Why didn't someone tell me on my first day?"

"That's easy," Colbert said. "The school gets paid according to how many students live through fourth Friday count, not how many teachers."

Mr. D. laughed. "Is that why most of you carry water bottles around in addition to your backpacks, your jackets, and your books?"

"Most of us do, but some of us carry the water to gain weight," Jake said. This was unusual because Jake rarely talked and never volunteered for anything.

"Like pumping water instead of iron? I hate to tell you Jake, but water weight isn't going to get you anywhere."

"Coach says I need to put on twenty pounds, and I went to a football clinic last summer and even the small college coaches said I needed thirty more pounds to even be considered. So I take this junk and you have to drink lots of water or it tears up your kidneys or something."

"What junk?"

"Mine's called Muscle Quick, but it's all ephedrine. Everybody on the team takes it."

"Where do you get it?

"Health food stores."

"Does your coach know?"

"Sure. He's the one who tells us not to use it, and that it's against league rules. Then he tells us to put on the weight and where not to buy the stuff. He sees the bottles."

"Everyone. Do you see the story here? In fact, lots of stories here?"

"I'm not saying anything against coach. I need to play every game and get a scholarship to get out of town," Jake said.

"No, I don't mean telling on the coach or running wires under your pads recording every word when he gives his famous Gipper speech before each game. No, let's find out all about this ephedrine and print it on our front page and let athletes make an informed decision. Also, let's find out what's in our water and how much weight the average student should carry in their back-pack."

All three stories ended up on our front page. Well actually the drinking fountain one wasn't a story, but we ran a big picture of a dead student on the floor by the drinking fountain. It was Kristen and she had her face painted up kind of white, we could have just used one of the Goths but didn't, and we stuck plastic roses on her chest. The cut line explained that we had sent water samples to the state and we would print the results of the tests in the next issue. We became fixated on wa-ter.

Ephedrine turned out to be bad stuff. Just the volume of water you had to drink actually increased the danger, and it was tough on more than just the kidneys. We ran a whole list of maybe eight problems, and Jake quit us-ing before the paper came out. Coach made another speech about how he didn't want any of his players tak-ing any of the ephedrine crap, but he complimented them on their constant hydrating.

Ten percent. According to some medical journal, a student isn't supposed to carry more than ten percent of their body weight on their backs unless the pack has a frame, and nobody at our school had a frame. We weighed a bunch of the packs, and some weighed over forty pounds. None of the girls would let us weigh them, but we didn't pick any four-hundred-pound girls to weigh. Mine was thirty-three pounds, and I'm not going to tell you what I weigh either.

CHAPTER 8
SECOND EDITION

Remember we already got in trouble for the "crap" thing so we tried to be extra careful. Let me tell you what wasn't in the second paper. Belger wasn't in the second paper, and Sean had the picture and everything. He was supposed to go the auditorium to take a picture of the Marching Band, which was going to play at half time at Notre Dame, and they were leaving that day. Yeah, them and 200 other bands.

Okay, so I'm not a big fan of high school marching bands. All the parents in the stands cheering for their sons or daughters who were probably freezing while playing their one note, flat, in "Flight of the Bumblebee," then back to football and all the good Catholic parents committing their kids to someday playing the saxophone for the green and gold or whatever color they wear at Notre Dame.

I was in band in middle school, but mostly all I did was my homework for other classes from the dreaded third row clarinets. The director had to know what we did back there, but as long as we looked like we were playing at the concerts and didn't actually play a note, he didn't care.

Okay so back to Sean and 'the picture.' Just as he

rounded the corner to the auditorium, here comes Belger out of the john and he's trailing this roll of toilet paper that is just bouncing along and streaming out twenty feet behind him. It's tucked into his pants.

Sean yelled, "Hey Belger," and Belger turned to look and he snapped the picture. Belger had this big grin and Sean caught it perfectly, shooting right down the line of toilet paper. By the time Belger got to Haverly's class, Sean was right behind him. Belger just walked right in and sat down as if he knew nothing of the now fifty feet of toilet paper running from the door, across the front past Haverly, and to the back left chair now containing an innocent looking Belger.

The class was roaring, and when Haverly looked up from his notes, he screamed at Belger to get out of his room and never come back. He was red and spitting.

Sean said, "You should have seen Belger. He jumped up as if he was seeing the toilet paper for the first time and said, 'Oh no! This is so embarrassing,' as if he were a Victorian gentleman. He pulled the toilet paper from his pants and started wadding it up as if to hide it, but it kept unraveling not getting any shorter, and the class roared."

Haverly screamed again for him to "Leave Now!" and Belger went running out of the room, feet flying sideways, flinging toilet paper, with Haverly screaming after him to go directly to Mr. Silvers' office.

Haverly was really all right. At least he tried to teach us, but I'll tell you, if his notes were any older or had any value at all, they'd go straight to the Smithsonian when he retires. Plus, Belger had mooned Bitely who I told you about earlier, right in front of her class last spring. She turned just in time to catch him. I was there. He had to finish the semester copying those stupid notes while sitting in the office. It made me want to moon her too if I could get the same deal, just so I wouldn't have to see her parading around in those short skirts of hers trying to look like one of the kids. Mrs. Robinson all the way. I didn't have the guts, I guess.

Silvers pulled a Silvers and Belger got nothing. He sent him right back to class because Belger stuck to the "so embarrassing" story; thus Silvers had no proof. I heard Haverly threw a fit. Dombrowski wouldn't let us run the picture, because it "might be hurtful for either Haverly or Silvers." I'll bet if we could have produced one last paper, Dombrowski would have let us put it on the front page.

Sean of course forgot all about taking the Marching Band picture, and Anna was all pissed at Sean because she wrote the story and was editing the school news page and wanted the picture. Sean called her anal-retentive, and she got all mad, and Sean would pout. I think if it wasn't Anna, at least one of the girls was always angry at Sean. I had my turns.

Another picture we never printed was Fredrich, the exchange student from Germany. Why Sean got the school camera more than anyone else I don't know, but Sean got Fredrich to wear this bright red This Bud's for Me and it didn't have a picture of a beer t-shirt and stand in the hall and talk to the principal while he took their picture. We have all kinds of rules for shirts like that, but they are only enforced by a few teachers. That was Sean's point. Silvers just put his arm around Fredrich's shoulder and smiled for the camera. In fact, Fredrich was holding a pop and that's against the rules too, though we sell it by the gallon in the cafeteria and at sporting events.

Dombrowski censored this picture saying he liked his job, and wouldn't run it in the next issue either when we ran the feature articles on the exchange students.

Kristen argued with him that this was just like seeing the senator take a bribe and for once, Dombrowski didn't have an answer, but Kristen let it go.

We had a hood surfing accident in the parking lot and that didn't get in the paper either. Nules and Jonesy were in the car. I really don't know either one of them, and I don't know their first names, which would be changed anyway, but I know they are two of the group who hang across the street smoking before school, during lunch, after school and anytime they skipped.

What a life. Jonesy was driving, with Husted surfing the hood. I guess Nules told Jonesy it would be funny if they slammed on the brakes so Jonesy did. There's a kid whose parents never should have started a family. Husted momentarily took flight until he crashed and burned on the pavement in front of the cafeteria. Old Nules and Jonesy had no idea what to do so they ran into the office yelling they found Husted knocked out in the parking lot and it looked like a hit and run. They were heroes on the six-o'clock news and everything, but by seven someone remembered the surveillance system and there were our heroes racing through the parking lot, slamming on the brakes, with Sted connecting on a half gainer with one-and-a-half-twist and no splash whatsoever. You can still see it on YouTube.

Dombrowski wouldn't let us run that either because he thought it glorified hood surfing, which it did. Sted did get a broken wrist, lost a tooth and punctured a lung, so he never got punished. Silvers made Nules and Jonesy park way down by the football field for the whole rest of the semester. That's like an extra ninety feet. I think they should have just neutered the whole mess of them.

We weren't allowed to call for the resignation of Siddle, the football coach even though we hadn't won a game yet. I didn't care one way or the other. Nobody on the paper really did except Jake. The more they lost the less chance he had of getting a scholarship. But it probably wasn't all Siddle's fault. Jake told us they had so few go out this year they were starting two freshmen who on a good year might be able to play JV. Dombrowski thought that high school sports should be about having fun and building character and not about winning, so as near as he could see, Coach Siddle was doing a fine job minus the ephedrine thing.

Erin wrote the "having fun, building character" sensitivity piece and it looked like something out of our handbook. I read that too. I had to do detention once when I had three tardies in a class. I had no homework and left the book I was reading in my car. One would think a detention room to have magazines or newspapers or something to read. All I found was a handbook, so I read it thinking maybe if I ever did go bad, I could use it for the loopholes like Belger. I think Erin believed the building character thing though. When I was a kid, I tried basketball, tennis, soccer and even volleyball, all the coaches were the same. Win, win, win. Never, what counts most as that we were the nicest losers in the gym.

Oh, and one more thing that didn't make the paper. The teachers settled their contract just after our first issue went out. Some of them had been picketing and most of them were wearing stickers about how teachers have value. Then they signed a new contract and everyone was friends again.

Sean told Dombrowski, "You have to have a genetic defect to be a teacher. They can be bought so cheap. Their raise didn't even cover inflation. My old man is a lawyer and my ma sells real estate, and I bet they make more in a month than you makes in a year. And it's not as if Dad has to orate in court or anything. He just tells rich people their tax breaks are legal.

"Looks good," Sean would say in a low all-knowing voice with his hands entwined behind his back. " Ten thousand dollars please."

Dombrowski said the contract was too old of news, but I think he knew Sean spoke the truth. It probably hit home every time he got in his rusting Oldsmobile, which they don't even make anymore, drove past all the nice houses in the immaculate subdivisions, and parked it behind my house in the place made for my grandma to die in. I'm not saying that all teachers are underpaid, but certainly Dombrowski, and Eggle in Psyche and Neihardt in Lit. were.

So what did make the paper? We sort of finished up that drinking water story. We got the results back from the state, and they said the water was drinkable with a little excess iron. That stuff was brown. Every morning it was brown. It didn't seem right, so I went online and checked out the test. I found the state's testing proce-dure was set in 1926 and hadn't changed since. They don't even look for most pollutants. I'm guessing half the pollutants didn't even exist in 1926. Mr. D. made me tell the whole class, which I didn't want to do but did.

Anna suggested we take a glass of water down to Stephans, the Chemistry/Physics teacher and have him find out what was in it. When we did he said we needed a spectrometer to see what's in the water. I asked if he had one, and he laughed and said he'd seen one once.

To find out what was really in our water, we needed to send it to a private lab, which cost almost one hun-dred dollars. We decided to start collecting pop bottles to raise the money for the test. There was no way the school board or Silvers was going to pony up for some-thing they didn't want the answer to. Every time I walked in that room after that, I could smell those cans and bottles fermenting. We should have washed them before cramming them into Dombrowski's cabinets and the boxes in the back of the room.

I wrote a small story about our water results and that we were going to raise money to get a real test. We had our first "Dear Abby" type column, which Kristen wrote. She was perfect for it, because as I said, she would say anything to anyone, especially about sex, which is really what every kid wants to know about.

One of Kristen's first "letters" that she wrote herself described a date rape. It had to be real. Dombrowski wouldn't let her print it saying it was too graphic, but he did promise the whole class that if we got a real letter like that, we would run it. Her other letters were about lousy boyfriends, a recurring theme for Kristen, fat, not a Kristen problem, and terminal shyness. No doubt that was for me. Bottom line, apparently, is I need a personality and some self-esteem. But Mr. D always said self-esteem is crap, and he wasn't going to create any more "M&M-soccer-trophy for participating kids."

The problem with our Entertainment Page was the movies were out of town by the time the paper was printed, and Sean was supposed to write a movie review or two. He wrote book reviews instead. He said, "The best movie review ever written was for a movie called, *Less Than Zero,* which said, "On a scale of one to ten, I'd give it less than zero." Concise. Perfect. Clean. So he reviewed *The Earth is Enough.* He said, "The book is enough. Read it."

You would have thought he started global warming right there in the classroom when Liz was pasting up that page and that's all she found. She got all red, called Sean a stupid abortion, and dragged Dombrowski over to the computer to see it.

He read the review and looked at Liz. "Have you read the book?"

"No."

"It's enough."

She glared at him. I think she thinks all males are in on some kind of anti-female conspiracy. "What will I do with all the empty space?"

"I'm sure if you ask Sean he will review some more books for you."

She turned and sneered at Sean like a little kid who tattled and won.

He relented and did a review for a Faulkner and a Kierkegaard, which nobody else in this school was ever going to read. Actually, the book review thing became kind of popular, and Sean had to write one for every future paper. Colbert gave him a book by Franklin Graham but we couldn't print the review.

CHAPTER 9
THIRD EDITION

The Abou, Taboo, Tattoo issue: and it was all mine. I was the editor despite telling Mr. Dombrowski I wasn't ready. He said, "There is no one in this class more ready for this job than you," and I felt kind of good and didn't fight it. But the problem was Bryan's fault. Or Mr. Silvers'. Certainly that nosey Mrs. Farroll, the superintendent's wife who was a secretary in the junior high. What did she care if we ran a naked butt on our front page? You couldn't tell. And everybody's seen butts.

Ever since Mr. Dombrowski moved into Grandma's house it became the class joke, whispering in my ear, "Have you seen him naked?" I say this because of the butt thing. I never saw his butt, but I know he wore boxers. He worked late into just about every night sitting in Gram's living room with a light on. I guess he was grading papers and reading books for his English classes. When it was hot he wore boxers and a t-shirt and never knew I was a lousy sleeper. What's one butt? The kids loved it. I think it was our best issue yet. The paper had been out two days when Mr. Silvers and Mr. Daniels, the janitor, came knocking on our door right at the beginning of the hour. Mr. Dombrowski had just gotten there after being outside, so he hadn't started his usual talking yet. All four of the computers were going because they always were. Kids came in early to work. They had to. The two ad teams were at the door waiting for Mr. Dombrowski to take roll and say whatever he was going to say.

When the two men came in, Mr. Daniels pushing a two-wheel cart, Mr. Dombrowski said, "Welcome to the newspaper class. I realize we're a little sloppy but I don't think you will need the cart." He smiled but it wasn't real.

"You might say we are here to clean up this class, Mr. Dombrowski," Mr. Silvers said. "We're here to clean up the obscenities you are printing."

"I don't know what you are talking about." Mr. Dombrowski looked around the class for answers. I think the stress was getting to him. He worked a lot. You have no idea how many days he stayed after school and worked on the paper, especially near deadlines. Some of us stayed and worked, and we usually didn't go home until six or later. A few times he bought pizza. And the newspaper already owed him seventy dollars after only two issues.

"Do you still have this month's issue of the *Water-GatePost*?" Silvers said it with a sneer. That was the moment I knew I hated him. I had always thought of Mr. Silvers as our version of the Wal-Mart greeter, because he never seemed to do anything except smile and say hi in the cafeteria and at sports events. Not that I went to many events but he was always there sucking up to the wealthy parents.

Mr. Dombrowski went to the corner and grabbed a copy from the stack. When he passed me he looked at me like, "What obscenity?" and I just shrugged my shoulders. I didn't know, even though, like I said, it was my paper.

Mr. Silvers looked past him and said to Mr. Daniels, "Make sure you get all of those, Jim," and Mr. Daniels rolled the cart to the back of the room and put maybe a dozen papers on it. "Do you have any more?" he asked looking at Mr. Dombrowski.

"We distributed them two days ago so no, but what is this all about?"

"That little picture you planted right on the front page."

They started to whisper a lot, or at least Mr. Silvers did. He showed the paper to Mr. Dombrowski and shielded it from our "virgin eyes." That's really funny with Kristen. And Jake. And Randy. And half the rest of this school. At least the juniors and seniors. We could see Mr. Silvers pointing to something on the front page, and we could all tell it was in Bryan's "Tattoo" article.

"That's a butt?" Mr. Dombrowski said it out loud.

"Yes it's a butt." Mr. Silvers was whispering but we could all hear it.

"How can you tell?"

"Because it's not on her leg. The article says the butterfly tattoo is on Barb Abou's leg, and you can go check. It's not there."

"I'm not going to check."

"Well you should have before you printed this paper."

"How do you know it's on her butt?" It was as if they had forgotten all about us. We were quiet enough, but I know I was dying to get out my paper and see the butt picture.

"Mrs. Farroll called. She was outraged. So I brought Miss Abou in for questioning. I put a little pressure on her and she told me it was on her butt. She offered to show me. She wanted to. I had Mrs. Budd check her and sure enough, that is a picture of her butt on the front page of your paper. Mr. Dombrowski, if you want to continue working in this district, you will get to the bottom of this."

Colbert started snickering, and then I caught the obviously unintended pun. Also, ironically, most of the students called Mrs. Budd Mrs. Butt, behind her back. Mr. Silvers remembered us again and took Mr. Dombrowski out into the hall. Since Mr. Daniels had already wheeled out his twelve copies, Randy pulled out his and we all gathered around. I guess you could see it was a butt, but there was no crack or anything. It looked as much like a leg as a butt.

Then, like magic, we all turned to Bryan. He was grinning and looking stupid at the same time. Kevin asked, "Is this Barb's butt?"

Bryan nodded and grinned.

"You mean she showed you her butt and let you take her picture?" He emphasized the "you."

"No, I drew it." This sarcasm was pretty gutsy for Bryan, especially around Kevin who picked on him constantly, but he seemed to see a new-found respect among his classmates.

"Watch it Weenie," Kevin said but even he seemed to appreciate a weenie who could get Abou to pull down her pants.

I was dying to know where he took the picture, but everyone kept asking stupid things like, "What else did she show you?" or "Did she have any other tattoos?" or "Anyone else show you anything?" which were pretty good questions I'll admit, but the answer was no. Finally Kristen said, "He actually took it at school, down by the gym, real quick, after last hour, which they shared."

About then Mr. Dombrowski came back in. We went silent to see his reaction. "We have a problem here guys. We seem to have offended some people. Running a newspaper is hard. Sometimes it is good to offend people or at least make them think about their positions. A good example of that would be Daryl's, Colbert's, editorial calling for the resignation of most of Congress and ceding Alaska back to the Russians. Thoughtful, well documented, and not a single complaint so far.

"Of course, no resignations so far either. Now this. It was clever, but probably stupid. In fact, I liked the two articles showing both sides of the tattoo craze. They were balanced and not glorifying. But Bryan," and here he turned and looked just at Bryan, but you could see the hurt on his face. "You had to know the sh—stuff was going to hit the fan when people figured out you took a picture of a student's butt and ran it on the front page of our paper. Mr. Silvers has not been a huge supporter of our paper so our continuation is tenuous at best. This jeopardizes everything we have done. We want people to respect us and actually consider our opinions relevant."

"Mr. Dombrowski?"

"Yes Kristen."

"Don't you think this is a tad over-reactionary? It's just a butt and not a particularly good one at that. Everyone has one."

"Probably. But not everyone has a butt on the first page of their paper, and what was the purpose of sneaking a butt on the front page if not to generate an over-reaction? We could have run one more arm, or ankle, or an actual leg. Bryan, can you answer that?"

"I thought it would be cool. Barb suggested it and I sure wasn't going to turn her down." Then, almost as an afterthought or closing arguments, "And you really can't tell it's a butt."

"But you had to know eventually it would come out.

Did you tell Lauren?"

"No. But she wouldn't have let me, and I just thought at most you would tell me never to do that again. And," he got a lot quieter here and looked at his desk. "I guess I thought it was cool too."

"Let me be honest with you Bryan, and I guess the whole class. Coolness is a matter of character and you all have a lot of character that will eventually be recognized by your peers." Then he smiled and looked straight at Bryan. "How would you like to go through life as Jake, with no redeeming character traits whatsoever?" Jake laughed out loud. "Or Matt? At least you've seen a girl's butt."

"I bumped a girl pretty hard in the hall the other day, Mr. Dombrowski," Matt said.

"That's practically a date, Matt. We're getting closer all the time."

"You'll get me there."

"So, Mr. Dombrowski?"

"Yes," again Kristen.

"Since you are being so honest. If you were Bryan and some girl let you take a picture of her butt, would you have snuck it in your school newspaper?"

"Wow. It's questions like that that get me in trouble. Can I just say we didn't have a school newspaper?"

"No." Half the class said that.

"Okay, but this doesn't leave this room. That picture would have been the highlight of my life, and I would have gotten it into the paper if it took a Watergate style break-in."

The whole class exploded into a bunch of "I knew it," and "You're okay Mr. Dombrowski," but he stopped it. "This is different though. This is a very conservative town and a very conservative administration. I lived in a town run by a bunch of ex-hippies who never grew out of that whole free-love sixties stuff." I don't think Mr. Dombrowski realized it at the time but this one act solidified the class against Mr. Silvers. Us against him. Good versus evil.

"What's Silvers going to do to us?" Erin asked.

Sean answered, "He won't do anything."

"Actually," Mr. Dombrowski said, "we have to go to every room and ask for the papers back."

Lots of "What" and "That's insane."

Mr. Dombrowski sort of sighed. "No ads. No news. No other work today. We are going to fan out through this entire building and ask every student in every class for our papers back."

"What if they want to know why we want them back?" Kevin asked.

"That's a problem. We can say we're encouraging recycling. Pair up and bring them back."

A student in the first room Kristen and I went to asked the question and Kristen immediately said, "Cause Abou's butt is on the front page."

Nobody gave them up. I think the other pairs answered similarly because the only group that brought back any papers at all was Liz and Travis, who always do what they are told, and they only brought back four. Mr. Stengg told us in his PE class that Mr. Silvers ordered a confiscation of any papers in students' possession. Like Sean always says, "Stupid, stupid, stupid."

My issue became the most sought after paper, and when I went to the senior graduation open houses, I almost always saw a copy on the table mixed in with the trophies, pictures, and other education paraphernalia. And Bryan became a lot more "cool," and Abou, while she was always pretty popular, she just skyrocketed in the eyes of the guys.

In case you didn't know, Abou rhymes with taboo

and I'm sure it was Kristen who first called the paper the Abou, taboo, tattoo issue. And you know Bryan's articles were really well done. That's why I put them on the front page. He had six pictures of tattoos. He interviewed a tattoo artist, several students who had tattoos, a guy in alternative ed. who tattooed himself and friends using an electric pen he made with a motor from a model car, and a doctor who removes tattoos. The doctor was a relative, but he didn't say that in the story. The butt should have offended no one. Lord knows, if there were any virgin eyes in this school they were mine, and I wasn't offended.

Silvers came the next day to get the rest of the papers, and he wasn't happy when we only gave him three. Matt took one. He said he wasn't here when they were distributed. I still have the six at home I took the first day, and no one will ever take them from me. I'm proud of that paper. Silvers made us put out a box in the hall for more papers to be returned. We called it our recycling box, but all we ever got was garbage and unneeded homework.

He came back the next day again. This time he wanted to see Colbert. Colbert just trudged behind him back to the office, wearing his little bow tie. He returned about fifteen minutes later and I had never seen him so excited or happy, and we went to elementary together. He closed the door, looked around to see that everyone was listening, and said, "Guess what. He thinks I'm a Communist."

"Did he say that?" Mr. Dombrowski asked.

"Mostly he asked about my parents and who they voted for. Silvers said, 'Republican, Democrat, Communist? You know young man, I do recognize sarcasm,' Your rants and little bow ties do not fool me. He said Democrat are just like Communists. It was hilarious. I gathered he had finally quit looking at Abou's butt and read my editorial. I told him I was a Republican all the way, that's why I wear this tie and it's red, white and blue. So, he asked, 'then why did you write this?' and pointed to my article. And I said, "Did you read it? I can help you with the big words.'"

"You didn't really say that did you?" Mr. Dombrowski asked.

"Oh, but I did." Mr. Dombrowski covered his eyes. "Silvers turned red and assigned me five days of in-school detention. I said, 'good, that will give me lots of time to work on my next editorial calling for your resignation.' He called me insolent, which was a pretty good word, and I asked him if it was true that he only gave Peterson two days detention for putting laxative in Ms. Joppa's coffee, and now I get five for insulting him." Colbert stood there grinning like he had just checkmated the pope.

"Daryl. Colbert, I have no doubt that you are right on all issues but insulting him isn't going to help us."

"I'm sorry Mr. Dombrowski, but he was wrong and I just couldn't hold back. I don't want to hurt the class or you. It is my First Amendment right to speak out and I don't care if this is just a little school paper that hardly anyone reads. I have things to say."

"You are right, but yet, he holds power over you as evidenced by the detention."

"Socrates took his poison and I will take my detention."

"Yes, but what comes after the detention?"

"A life sentence?"

Needless to say, once Bryan and Colbert pulled their little stunts, any hope of getting new computers was over, though I don't think they were ever ordered. Silvers hated us and all we ever did was work and put out the best paper this school ever saw. I learned more in this class than I ever thought possible. I wrote articles. I took pictures and pasted up pages. I interviewed people, sold ads and used graphic programs. Yes, I really could interview people by the end. I even recognized and fixed common computer problems. The only thing I couldn't do was fathom why the school didn't support a class like this and a teacher like Mr. Dombrowski. So we went conservative on the Christmas Edition.

CHAPTER 10
CHRISTMAS EDITION

The blah, blah, blah, humbug edition. Okay, so it was a Christmas edition, spread the holly and hang the good cheer and all that, but we purposely made it especially blah, very blah. This time it was Colbert's term as managing editor. I think Dombrowski gave him the job as penance.

Colbert actually got more animated as the paper progressed. Five days of detention meant he had to do his newspaper work after school and leave us all notes. Sometimes we brought articles to him in detention, and I know he asked Kristen if she could sneak him in a file, the metal kind.

"They never built a prison that could hold Colbert!" He had reverted to speaking in third person. He flashed two V's with his fingers to everyone who walked by. No one ever knew what that meant until he returned and told us that it meant, "I am not a crook. You know. From the greatest Republican of all." But we didn't know. We did know he didn't dare wear that stupid bow-tie in detention. That would be like wearing a meat suit to the circus.

He told the whole class he asked a teacher he trusted, code named Debbiedoesdallas since Woodward and

Bernstein used Deepthroat, and Debbiedoesdallas said don't investigate Silvers because you can't print anything anyways.

Debbiedoesdallas said, "He's just a good ol' boy putting in his time until he retires. Most of them are, and as long as they say the right things in public, win enough games, shake enough hands, and control the school board, nobody cares."

He thought the whole thing would have been a lot cooler if they had met in an abandoned parking garage or a farm, seven rows of corn in. Dombrowski told him Debbiedoesdallas was probably right and not to ask any more teachers about Silvers, and Colbert agreed.

So we cooled it and wrote Christmas stories, features on the exchange students, some light-hearted fare on the girl's volleyball team, and even finished up our story on the drinking water in our school. We had to "nice" that down too. It turns out our water is full of junk from really bad pipes. The lab recommended avoiding drinking it if possible. Any other edition and we would have headlined our paper, MONTE-SILVER'S REVENGE, or JOURNAL UNCOVERS FOUL ADMINISTRATION PLOT TO KILL KIDS. But it must have killed Colbert to write: DRINKING WATER SOMEWHAT UNHEALTHY. But he did it for Mr. Dombrowski.

The funniest part of the paper was JJ's Jumper cartoons. I don't know if I told you about JJ. Erin found him. He was always doodling or drawing cartoons, so she asked Dombrowski if he could draw for the paper even though he wasn't a member of the class. His sense of humor was darker than Sean's, and this time he drew these suicide guys standing at the edge of buildings and bridges and stuff. In the Christmas issue, he had a Rabbi trying to talk the guy down. He starts with, "You think you got problems..." and by the time it is done the

Rabbi jumps and the other guy changes his mind. I guess you have to see it 'cause all the expressions are real cool and stuff. The other cartoon had this kid on a bridge who was obviously stoned and he jumps shouting, "It's a bird, it's a plane, it's Superman." Just before he hits he has this sick look and says, "I really need to rethink this whole drug thing."

About a week after the paper came out, one of the sophomores did kill himself. It was terrible, but I didn't know him. He was Anna's cousin and she said he was always a little weird, but nice. I gathered their home-life was a mess, and there was a lot of innuendo that he was picked on a lot at school. Though JJ continued to draw cartoons for us, we never ran another Jumper cartoon and Silvers never said anything about it, but I'd bet he wanted to.

CHAPTER 11
"PILAR OF THE COMMUNITY"

This time it wasn't Silvers who blew up. It was Farrell, the superintendent. Kristen says he's a sleaze. Big time. Of course that might not be true at all because her aunt loves to tell stories, and I don't know him other than what he did to Dombrowski.

Kristen's aunt said Farrell once tried to pick her up in a bar in Green River, about two towns from here and her aunt is no prize. She used to dance at a strip club here, but there comes a time when you have to give that up and her time came and went. And then it went again. And still she danced. She says she knew who he was right away and chewed him out when he tried to pick her up.

Farrell kicked her son, Kristen's cousin Lou, off the football team when he got caught smoking under the stands after practice. Lou said there were six of them, including Farrell's son, but the coach only "recognized" Lou. Lou always did the little quote things in the air when he said "recognized." He still does and he's twenty-one now, spraying glass in the boat-works. Lou usually tells the truth without all the drama of his mother. He coughs all the time, and he blames the factory, but I doubt it because they wear these big masks and he chain smokes.

Kristen said she would like to believe her aunt about Farrell, but her aunt claims she slept with ex-president Gerald Ford on the fifty-yard line in Michigan stadium, Robert Redford when he was shooting *The Natural,* naturally, the Reverend Billy Graham against the pulpit of a small Baptist church in Arkansas while she was on vacation, and one of the Righteous Brothers, but she changes which brother depending on whom she is telling the story to. And Kristen said they're not really brothers at all, but I don't care since I don't know who any of them are except Ford, who did something stupid in office or something, and the others must be old. You should see her aunt. If Kristen thinks she is going down that road someday, no wonder she sleeps with guys now. Her aunt tells details you wouldn't believe and I wouldn't write.

So Farrell was really late getting mad at us. He probably never read our paper until the television crew showed up, which was about a week after the third paper came out. They wanted to do a story on the drinking water in the high school, and they interviewed a bunch of kids who all said they never drink it. Then they showed Silvers, who looked like a total idiot mostly because he is a total idiot. He went on about how we have fine water and how he drinks it all the time. They followed him to a drinking fountain where they proceeded to show his butt bent over the thing. That was funny, but he didn't look real quenched when he came up out of the thing either. There were several letters to the editor and a few moms showed up at the next board meeting where Farrell assured them that he was "looking into it," which everyone but a mom knows means "I ain't going to do crap."

It all blew away when Anna's cousin killed himself and there were a lot of special meetings making sure that never happened again. Basically, we had an extra counselor for a week, and the teachers had to be more vigilant. Students were supposed to see a teacher or counselor whenever one of their friends said they were going to kill themselves or started giving stuff away.

That would have filled the office if we had done that. I'm really not making fun of this situation because it was terrible, and something really good did come out of it. One of the teachers and one of the counselors made all the arrangements to set up a Challenge Day where a group came into the gym and challenged us to open up. I thought it was going to be 'high school stupid.' but it was amazing to line up in the gym and see how many crossed the line when they asked questions like: *Have you ever picked on other students? Were you abused as a child? Are either of your parents an alcoholic? Have you ever thought about killing yourself?* I won't tell you the questions I crossed over on, but I think I've been pretty sheltered compared to the rest of the kids.

I guess Farrell had a meeting with Dombrowski and was told we couldn't do any stories that might embarrass the administration or cost the school money, because the school was broke due to government cutbacks, and that the water tested good. So, we knew we weren't getting new pipes or drinkable water.

So, when Kristen's aunt called her mom and said she was getting free city water at her house and didn't even live in the city, her mom didn't believe her. Her mom had to pay almost six thousand dollars to hook up to water and sewer when she didn't even want them.

Kristen had to go to her aunt's one day to return some Tupperware from something or other her aunt had brought over. She was always running Tupperware to or from someone for her mom. It's like that is what she and her friends do, bake stuff for each other and have

Kristen return the Tupperware. It's much better now that she can drive. She used to have to carry it in the basket of her bike and hated when other kids saw her, or she had to deliver cupcakes without bouncing them so that the frosting stuck to the top of the lid. But her aunt was right. There was a straight line of dirt and patched sod leading from the road to her house, but not just at her house. The lines ran parallel to the road and then to every house in the neighborhood, same as our neighborhood when we got hooked up.

So Kristen asked her how she liked her new water and she said, "It tastes just like water, Sugar." She calls almost everyone Sugar, although it comes out "Shuga," like she's some kind of Southern Belle, which of course she's not. But she's really not fake with it either. She just does it and it works for her. She told Kristen KSR Industries paid for the whole thing. One of the workers told her, and he was supposed to be "kind of cute and someone you might want to get to know a little better if you ever get the chance."

Kristen assured her that she was doing okay on her own in that department. Her Aunt just wanted to tell her not to make the same mistake she made and like an idiot Kristen asked her, "What mistake?" She told her about some guy who kept asking her to her high school prom, and she finally gave in and went but never dated him again because he just wasn't much fun and truthfully not a lot to look at. Now he supposedly runs this billion dollar software company, Kristen said all the hints were Bill Gates, so she's supposed to find someone like him. Watch out Matt if she ever starts listening to her aunt.

So, the next day in newspaper class, she told the class about her aunt, but not the part about her being a dancer and all. Just the water part. Dombrowski thought we should check into it. It was unusual but he had certainly heard of corporations that did wonderful things for their communities including an ironworks, which gave a local high school a community pool.

This was where I became the third wheel. All of a sudden—remember Anna and Randy—we had to do things in groups of threes, which seemed reasonable, except I often was number three as in least intrusive. Kristen called the city's water department from school and identified herself like Dombrowski taught us. It was kind of cool because she often gets taken for an airhead, and this lady treated her like a professional reporter and said she knew nothing about it and that I needed to talk to Mr. Sadler, the director, "...who was not in today but she would leave him a message."

Randy volunteered and called KSR. That surprised all of us. He was transferred to Mr. John Bunting who was the public relations director for KSR. Instead of answering our questions on the phone, Mr. Bunting invited us to tour the plant with him.

We had called him on a Wednesday and the three of us visited on Friday. It was funny because Silvers had already heard we were going and talked to Dombrowski.

"They are just following up on an innocent story and aren't looking to write up anything negative about 'KSR, a pillar of our community,'" Mr. D. assured him.

Mr. Sadler still hadn't called Kristen back and she left the school's number and my cell number.

It had snowed on the Friday we visited and everything was covered in white, like a sheet draped over the whole industrial complex. There were a lot of cars in the parking lot, all white though, and the lot was tracked with parallel lines as if made by a giant Spiro graph. I always like snow. There were mounds off to the side in an apparently vacant lot that Randy pointed to and said they were old machines. I think he was expecting to see pipelines pumping black sludge running into formerly pristine creeks, and fifty-five-gallon drums with skull and crossbones painted on the sides leeching their poison into Bambi and Thumper's habitat. But they were just old machines and Kristen told Randy if they were actually doing anything wrong they'd never invite us here to see it. Plus, anyone driving by, like the city inspectors or someone, could see anything they were doing illegally.

So we walked in and a really friendly lady greeted us. It was kind of a small waiting room like for a doctor, only nicer, but with no magazines to read. That was okay because I never know what to read at the doctors. The *Better Homes and Gardens* don't interest me, and I wouldn't want anyone to see me reading *Seventeen* with some airbrushed actress bragging about losing twelve pounds in three minutes on a new super-diet.

The lady told us that Mr. Bunting had run a quick errand and would be right with us. Do you know what the quick errand was? Milk and Cookies. Windmill cookies. For us. Like some kind of after-school-treat for elementary kids. So much for professionalism. I thought it was cute, but afterwards Randy said he wanted to puke. Of course, he and I ate a bunch of cookies because we could dip them. Kristen only drank the milk.

Mr. Bunting shook our hands and led us into a dark-wooded room with a big table and cushy chairs. I loved the chairs. How come schools don't use chairs like that? I could hear the bell ringing and kids moaning because they didn't want to get up, go home, and leave their chairs.

The room itself had plaques and trophies attesting to the company's quality and support of area softball teams. There were chrome axles, window trim and door latches neatly lined up on shelves. Mr. Bunting told us these were just a small part of what KSR manufactures for the auto industry. He stacked us up with pamphlets attesting to KSR's seventy-fifth anniversary. Their Quality One rating for Ford. Their projected earnings for stockholders, board of directors, and market share on said door latches. How many jobs KSR provided for the community and in turn, how many other jobs those jobs led to. We must have gotten a dozen pamphlets but none looked like they mentioned water.

Randy spoke up. "Is KSR paying for the water hook-ups in Shadyside Subdivision, where Kristen's aunt lives?

Now Bunting was good and worth whatever KSR was paying him. He started with, "Well, you know there are almost sixty homes in that subdivision including eleven owned by employees of this company. Many of them can walk to work, which we actually encourage. Anything to save the environment. Well, we were running a new water main out to a new electrical generating plant we are partnering, along with some other businesses in the community. Warren Riegle, our CEO, said as long as we are running by those houses, let's hook them up. He's a very generous man always helping his employees and the community." Bunting even added, "Did you know he has a scholarship available at your school? Maybe you ought to apply and one of you might get it."

"What does it cost to run the water to Shadyside?" asked Kristen.

He said, "It really was pretty minor. Just one of the things Warren does for his community. The real story for your paper is jobs. We have over 400 employees in this town and kept them all busy during the last recession. We laid-off no one and our pay scale is one of the highest in town. We plan on growing by twenty percent over the next four years. This is a great town to live in and a great company to work for."

Randy acted as if he couldn't wait to get out of there. He had pamphlets in one hand and shook Bunting's hand with the other saying he had a test the next hour, which was a lie because he was in my class.

When we got outside to the car, Kristen asked him, "What's going on?

And Randy said, "I'm not going to listen to anymore of Bunting's crap."

"What crap?"

"Everything Bunting said is crap."

I asked him, "How do you know?

"I just do and will someday prove it."

Kristen and I thought Mr. Bunting was nice. Then Randy hit the gas way too hard and we kind of slid into a curb on account of the snow and had to back off it. Randy got even madder and the car went bumpity, bumpity, bumpity all the way back to the school.

I was in the backseat feeling ill.

CHAPTER 12
FOURTH EDITION

On Monday, Randy and Kristen and I came to class and told all about our meeting with John Bunting from KSR. Randy was still angry because he'd bent a sixty-dollar tie-rod tearing out of there and then blamed that on all the crap Bunting had fed them.

Kristen still thought Bunting was nice and that maybe they should do a story on how KSR provided water for the whole neighborhood without charge, even though Bunting had acted like it was no big deal. The two of them got kind of angry at each other.

"I won't do a PR piece for that company," Randy said.

"It might help the school paper since the administration always seems so mad at us," said Kristen.

The rest of us were just kind of sitting back enjoying the show when Dombrowski interrupted.

"Friends, Reporters, Classmates. Lend me your ears. Are we here to praise KSR or to bury them?"

The class was kind of shocked because Dombrowski jumped right on his desk and was holding his Sharpie as if it were a sword. I think this was from *Julius Caesar*. He did that stuff all the time. One time when Sean was kind of dozing and Dombrowski whispered, "Sean,

Sean. Where for art thou Sean?" He was holding an old dead carnation from homecoming just about straight in Sean's face. Sean jerked up and he had drool on his shirt and sputtered that he wasn't sleeping. We never knew what Dombrowski was going to do in that class, but he had fun, and Sean never slept in there again.

When he had everyone's attention he said, "We aren't here to 'get' anyone. Our job, our purpose, is to report the news people want or need to know in an unbiased manner." He looked at Randy. "Randy, you seem angry, probably too angry for the little bit of information they gave you." Randy shrugged. "And Kristen," he turned to her. "What kind of company hooks up an entire neighborhood to city water without charging them and then wants no credit in the paper?"

Dombrowski climbed off his desk and talked very quietly. "Look, we may have a big story here or we may have nothing. I think we should follow it but very carefully. Every fact will need two pieces of evidence to back it up. KSR is huge in this town. They probably did nothing wrong, but that whole lack of publicity thing is suspicious. Some people will probably hate us just for asking questions about KSR. It's almost like questioning the value of the Patriot Act or the Second Contract with America. Know anything about that Colbert?"

"I could never question either, sir," Colbert said. "I love the Patriot Act and would put video cameras in every girl's locker room if that's what it takes to stop Al Qaeda."

"Too late Colbert," Kristen piped in. "I'm already pregnant with Bin Laden's baby."

Sean asked if we could print that and Dombrowski got us back to the paper.

We talked to Anna about how this edition was shaping up and if there was going to be room for a big story.

Probably not, she said. "We can only run something if it's small, and I have to know pretty quickly."

That is really one of the problems with a high school paper. It takes a month to get one out and if a real story comes up, you have to wait another month to print it.

"Kristen," Dombrowski asked. "Did you ever hear back from the city?"

"No."

"You need to follow up on that. Randy, why are you so angry with KSR? How do you know this isn't just a goodwill gesture?"

"Look, Bunting lied," Randy said. "My grandpa worked there for twenty-two years and was laid-off almost three years ago. He and a bunch of his friends. Bunting told us KSR didn't lay anyone off. What they do is they say there is a shortage of orders, and then lay off the older ones like my grandpa who got paid more. Within a few days they hire new guys so they still have their 400 employees. My grandpa thought they'd never do it to him because he helped fight the UAW when the union tried to organize them back in the early nineties. Now Gramps works at Wal-Mart. Half the pay, half the hours, and no benefits."

"Though I appreciate your honesty, I'm not sure you can be unbiased enough for this story." Dombrowski said.

I put that quote in here because a lot of people said afterwards that we were just out to get KSR. That wasn't true, but I do kind of think we were out to get someone going all the way back to *All the President's Men.* Dombrowski really did say it though.

He told Randy, "Talk to your Grandpa about KSR if something comes of the story and we need some background. But otherwise you're off the story because a paper can never be vindictive."

I used 'vindictive' on my mother that night and was told to grow up.

So, we had to begin working on the KSR story while finishing that month's paper. We did some really cool stuff. That was the Globetrotters edition. Everyone saw it because ours was ten times better than the regular town paper. The Harlem Globe Trotters came to the Civic Center and we got to do exclusive interviews. It was Dombrowski's idea. He thought if we made arrangements well in advance they'd be happy to talk to us. We thought they'd be like rock stars, and you'd need backstage passes, and then they'd be all stoned trying to pick up Kristen or Erin.

But the Globetrotters didn't even try. They were real. They answered everything we asked and seemed really sincere about helping kids in every community. They'd get tired of the road and would like to change some of their tricks, but the audience expected certain things of them including the bucket of confetti which had long ago lost its fun for them.

They missed their wives and their children who rarely travel with them. They got paid well, but not one of them drove anything really cool. One of them said he drove a Prius and Sean said that must be his wife's car, and he said she has one too. Half their gate receipts go to local charities. In our town that meant the Women's Resource Center, so Wayne did a story on them too, but he couldn't take any pictures. It was good for Wayne.

Sean did a review on the *Twilight* series and *The Hunger Games*. Some of the girls were really irritated when he wrote about the *Twilight* books. "The first book could have been written by her little sister on a bad afternoon during a full eclipse with a power outage." He seemed not to like them but I am noting that he read them all.

Kristen did her columns, and I, yes me, started a product review of all the fast food restaurants in town. I got the idea because of those pictures on YouTube of the McDonalds hamburger that won't rot. So we placed one on top of the file cabinet, took its picture and vowed to include a new picture each month to see if it rotted or attracted flies. I actually thought their hamburger was okay, but when you got up into their meal deals, they were expensive, fattening, and I felt guilty before I even finished.

The next two days were big. Kristen and I went to Shadyside without Randy just to see what we could learn. Randy told us before we left that KSR was not working on their Boy Scout merit badges. This was like real reporting and I was excited.

Even though Kristen's aunt knew nothing, the lady across the street had plenty to say. She was wheeling her garbage down the driveway and I bumped Kristen so she would see her and say something. Kristen asked her about the water, and that lady just pointed to her cut up lawn and told us to follow it, see where it leads, and then come back and talk to her. So we did and found that it ended at the end of the subdivision. No big deal, but we went back to see the lady, Mrs. Fortuni. She was loud and talked with her hands, and Grandma would have said she was just being Italian.

"So what did you two learn?" We didn't have a clue. "Did you notice the pipeline ends right at the end of our sub, two blocks north of here?" She pointed. We nodded. Even Kristen didn't know how to deal with a truly crazy lady who spoke almost nose to nose.

"So where is the power plant they said they were running the water to? Did you find the end maybe in Danfield's back yard or in Pleva's garage?" We couldn't leave. It would be rude and we didn't have a story yet. So we stood there nodding and shaking until suddenly Fortuni grabbed me by the arms. "Can't you see? They poisoned us."

It was the weirdest thing. The next day in class I told everyone. I stood in front of the class. I couldn't stop: it was the coolest story. Everyone kept looking at me like 'Whot is that?' Did that crazy lady rub off on her? "I didn't know if I should jump off her porch or what. I mean, sure it was rude, but she really grabbed me, and I thought she was crazy, and if I did jump, she might have fallen over and she was old."

I kept talking faster and faster. Kristen told me afterwards maybe I had been bottling that up for the last seventeen years.

"I thought she was going to start shaking me, like one of those Steven King movies where her eyes roll back or turn red. But she just held me as if we were supposed to agree with her that she had been poisoned by KSR just because she had said it. But I stood there just shocked, and Kristen didn't do a thing, so I asked her who poisoned her and how did she know it. And she said, 'It all adds up. There are at least six families in this neighborhood now with cancer, and Herb, my husband, died from throat cancer eighteen months ago, and three young men, three, have Lou Gehrig's disease. Do you know what the odds of that are?'

"It was like she wanted an answer, and I was never that good at math and wouldn't have had a clue where to begin, so I said that I didn't know, and she told us it was over one in a billion. She said billion, right Kristen?" Kristen kind of just nodded like she was back with Mrs. Fortuni.

"She kept holding me, and then she looked me in the eyes again and said, 'It's in the water.' The poison, I asked. 'Yes, she said. What do you think I've been talking about?' How do you know it's KSR, I asked, and she said, 'Why else would they be giving us free water,' which made sense if you thought about it at all."

Sean started snickering here, but Kristen shot him a really freezing look and he shut up.

"Mrs. Fortuni told us that she had been complaining for years about the taste of the water, how it didn't taste like it used to, but no one would listen to a little old lady. Then when Herb, her husband, and you could really tell that she missed him and loved him, got sick, she complained all the more but nothing.

"It took her husband four years to die. She still hasn't paid all the bills because all she gets is Social Security and Medicare. She said when she dies, which she said shouldn't be too long now even though she hasn't gotten the cancer yet, they can sell her house and use it to pay Herb's bills. She didn't have any kids and was glad because of what the water might have done to them. I think this was about when she let go of my arms, which were sore and red by this time." I looked at Kristen who nodded again in confirmation and I noticed everyone was looking at my arms.

"So, Kristen asked her why she made us drive to the end of the pipeline if the power plant isn't there. 'That's the whole point. The new plant is in the city. South and west of here. Why would they take a pipeline from the city, run it north and east into the township if they wanted to go south and west?'"

"I told you guys!" Randy just burst in interrupting me, so I didn't talk anymore. That was it. Kristen told Randy to shut up so I could finish, but I kind of just backed up so that I was half behind Kristen and didn't say another word even when they asked.

Kristen finally said, "That was about all Mrs. Fortuni said, so we hopped back into Abigail, parked in the student parking, which should have reserved spaces for seniors, hustled our butts in our size seven shoes, and barely got to third hour on time." Dombrowski winced and I just wanted to disappear. "Can we write it up?"

"Let's see," he said. "You have a lady who is a great character but may or may not be crazy saying her water is poisoned. She talks of all kinds of illnesses, a water pipe that goes in the wrong direction and a government that doesn't listen. Sounds like a story."

"So is it or isn't it?"

"Back at you. Is it or isn't it?"

"If it's true it is."

"Exactly. Prove it one way or the other. Maybe parts of it are and others aren't. Find out which is which, and you might have a great story. Good work."

Kristen just about beamed. I've been in many classes with her and I never saw her care about any of her classes except newspaper. And truthfully, it really wasn't much like a class. I looked forward to it every day, as did most of the kids. It was weird. I'm not going to say it wouldn't have worked without Dombrowski because we can't know, but it worked with him.

CHAPTER 13
GRANDMAS AND GRANDPAS

S o at last we were doing something real. We agreed as a class not to discuss our KSR investigation. We said we didn't want to get scooped by the regular paper, but what was left unsaid was KSR was powerful enough to tell Ferrell to tell Silvers to tell Dombrowski we couldn't investigate them. Mrs. Fortuni was great. She set us on the right path or at least got us organized. Initially only four students were to investigate or report on KSR, because we still had a regular paper to put out, but eventually I think almost everyone was involved. Everyone certainly volunteered and wanted to play a part.

Kristen kept calling that guy from the city and he just never called back. We had all we were ever going to get from Mrs. Fortuni, and Mr. Bunting was obviously not paid to tell a bunch of kids the truth. So Colbert went his own route, kind of like the rest of his life. It was probably about two or three days after I got carried away and Colbert came into class all excited. You know those cartoon clowns on TV who get all excited and their bow-ties spin. That was Colbert. He kept looking out the door to see when Dombrowski was coming in. He walked him in the door and began.

"My mom has a friend who works for the city. Now I'm always going to refer to her as a her, but that doesn't necessarily mean she's a she." A bunch of us snickered, which only set Colbert to way over-explaining the situation. "Look, referring to her as a her but not meaning she was a her or a he, will be a lot easier doing that than using my hands to do the 'quote' thing. Which of course he did. "And she," doing the quote thing here, "really isn't a friend of my mom. So she wouldn't meet me at work or even talk to me there, but she talked. I won't even tell you where we met, but I'm sure no one ever saw us or suspected anything."

Kevin said, "Cougar," and Colbert just ignored him, too impatient to respond.

"We made these agreements to call her," quote things "a her," again "and a friend of my mom before she would tell me anything." One of his hands grabbed the other so they would stop doing that whole quote thing. "She asked me what I knew and I told her. She said I didn't know squat. It makes her sound tough, and I think that's how she wanted to sound, but she let me know that if I used her name or any information she gave me without corroborating sources, she could lose her job if not worse.

"No one from KSR or the city could ever know who she was. I agreed to it and told her I wouldn't even tell Mr. Dombrowski, and she thought that was best. Then she gave me just a rough outline of what took place. She said she would only outline it because that would make us work harder to dig up the facts which I could print."

"She said it probably began back in the forties or maybe even the late thirties when KSR was building parts for the war effort. Nothing KSR did at that time was illegal or even unusual. People thought the earth was just a giant sponge and you could dump anything anywhere you wanted and not hurt anything. So KSR did.

"All their chemicals and coolants that were spoiled or used or whatever, they just dumped them. Some in barrels, some just on the ground. She asked me if I ever played Little League and I said yeah, but I hated it with all that standing around. She gave me a funny look as if who wouldn't like Little League and then told me I was playing on top of one of KSR's dump sites. They capped it with clay and donated it to the children of the city. A hell of a legacy for our children, huh?

"I was taking notes by then and she asked me to stop. She said, 'No notes. You need to find your proof else-where.' She was just trying to help the people who live around KSR, especially those who live in Shadyside. She had heard there was a mess of illness there. By the sixties everyone knew it was unsafe to just dump their chemicals, but KSR kept dumping into the seventies and even the mid eighties. No one stopped them be-cause they are powerful in this town. Do you know what the loss of 400 jobs would mean to a town this size? All they have to do is threaten to move south and they can have whatever they want or do whatever they want. Plus, Warren Riegle, the president of KSR is the lead-ing Republican fundraiser in this half of the state.

"I'm telling you, when she said that I nearly died. No not the Republicans. This would give a whole new meaning to trickle down economics. I might have missed a few things she said here 'cause my mind was kind of picturing trickle down sludge moving into poor neighborhoods. When I caught back up with her she was saying something about the water-table flowing directly from KSR's backdoor dump site to Shadyside, and that was just one of many dump sites.

"She said KSR had already lost in court but had no intention of paying for the cleanup. I didn't even know what a water-table was. I looked it up last night in Wikipedia. It's real complicated but just understand they are underground aqua-firs where we get our drinking water.

"There was no way I was going to ask her any technical questions and look stupid. So I asked her if she had any papers that proved all this. It turns out that was stupid. She wondered what my mom had raised. She said that was the point. She wasn't going to give us anything that could lead back to her. We have to find the papers to prove that KSR had effectively poisoned the people living in Shadyside and probably several other neighborhoods. She gave me the worse look and asked, 'Now are you capable of doing this without getting me in trouble?'

"By the time I left her, she was okay. Our goal is to prove what she said without using her as a source. She assured me the evidence was there but we have to find it. So, that's us. We need to find the papers. I don't know if she's suggesting we break into city offices at night or what."

"Hold on Colbert," Mr. Dombrowski stopped him. "You did great, but breaking into offices is not going to happen. I know how your mind works. All in black. Middle of the night. Maybe you and Erin and Kristen and Lauren and Anna. Sound close so far?"

"Sounds good Mr. D."

"You guiding them against the dark halls, stepping over laser burglary systems, night vision goggles, holding hands maybe?"

"Even better," but Colbert was starting to turn red.

"Plant some bugs? Crack the safe? Pulitzer Prize? Man of the year?"

"Okay I get it, but a guy can dream can't he?"

"Yes a guy can dream, but a guy can't do anything illegal in here."

"Maybe Matt could break into their computers from right here," Sean threw in.

"Still illegal."

"And no girls." Kristen of course.

This is kind of weird here, but I think it is important. Grandma always told me if you can remember your dreams, they are trying to tell you something. So that night I dreamed I was in class and Colbert was telling his story only he was using a microphone and it was loud, real loud. I was covering my ears and everyone kept turning around and staring at me.

We had broken into the offices and Mr. Daniels, the janitor, had to wheel in all the evidence, just like he wheeled out the Abou Tattoo papers. Dombrowski was presenting Colbert with a huge gold star that looked like it was made from cardboard and covered in wrapping paper.

Suddenly Gram drove right into the classroom in a big red Cadillac convertible with fins and no one but me noticed, like that sort of thing happened every day. I tried to run to her but I couldn't move very quickly at all, and she waved me back to my seat.

"I'm here for him," she said and pointed to Dombrowski. "And get some clothes on Lorn." I looked down and I was naked and woke up.

I'm sure there's some truth in that dream somewhere. Instead, Mr. Dombrowski was emphatic that we do nothing illegal. We had to find our information legally. This was when Randy came in late and he was spitting mad.

"Sorry. Someone hid my shoes in my effing gym class. I take showers afterward, unlike the queer little wall-leaners who don't do anything but look for a chance to eff with those of us who actually do something in that class. I wanted Physics. I got PE. Schedule conflict. Stupid school."

I know what he was talking about, but I leaned every chance I got. In the girl's locker-room, all they did was steal your money, which I guess is worse than hiding your shoes, but not by much. I think Randy was so mad because he had stuff to tell us and Colbert was up front. This was supposed to be Randy's day.

"I talked to my Grandpa last night," Randy started while standing next to Colbert. "Lauren's crazy lady might be right. Everything out there might be poison. The first ten or twelve years he worked there, they had one guy, Miller, whose job every Friday was to dispose of barrels of chemicals. Most of them went to the dump but if the dump was closed or they had some that were supposed to be incinerated, which was really expensive, he was told to just dump them out back or in the swamp by the airport. It was his job and nobody ever thought anything about it. Everyone just assumed the chemicals went away. He even said the ballfields where we played Little League were a KSR dump-site, but that was before Grandpa's time at KSR. But he did see them cover it up. It didn't surprise him at all that now people were dying because some of the chemicals you weren't even supposed to breathe let alone drink. Miller died a long time ago, but Grandpa couldn't remember what he died from."

Wow. We were stunned. It was quiet and nobody said anything as we realized we had a real story. Up until then I think it was a fantasy. Dombrowski finally broke it.

"We need to be cautious, careful, quiet, and legal. Everything must be an absolute. No second-hand facts. Everyone do ads today, or columns or something safe, while I find out what to do next."

And everyone scrambled to look busy, but mostly we talked to Randy and Colbert.

CHAPTER 14
FREEDOM

Talk about pouting children. I think Randy was upset because he didn't get to be the first to tell the story, and Colbert was whiny because he wasn't the only one to tell a story. They both wanted all the attention, and I think Dombrowski had Colbert nailed when he teased him about breaking into City Hall with the girls in the class. I liked that I was included with Kristen and Erin, but not so much Anna. And if I was going to do something illegal, which I'm not, it wasn't going to be with Anna.

Mr. D had done his homework and he lectured the class on the Freedom of Information Act, or FOIA for short. He told us this was another one of the LBJ bills designed to make government less secretive. We could fill out a form and as long as the information we wanted wasn't a government secret or part of an ongoing suit, they had to give it to us. It seemed simple. So someone, I think it was Wayne, suggested we needed someone above suspicion, an innocent, and everyone kind of turned to Bryan. He was too innocent to know he was innocent.

Kevin whispered to Erin, "We can slide him in through the mail slot at night and forget the FOIA."

I heard him. Mr. D heard him. And more importantly Erin, the other innocent, said to Kevin, "That's not nice." Mr. D told Kevin to stay after class. Then Erin said she'd be willing to go with Bryan tomorrow if he wanted her to. Colbert and Randy both volunteered to be the third person. But the class decided Colbert might run into his source, and Randy would make it appear like we were out to "get" KSR, which of course we were by that time, but didn't ever admit it as a class. So Mr. D asked if I would go along. Third wheel again. I wondered if I'd be stuck in the back seat again.

The next morning I met Erin right after Chemistry. First hour Chemistry should be illegal, especially if you have something cool to do second hour. It goes like a month. That day it went like a year. Erin wasn't happy either. She had Spanish II first hour, and the teacher threw a surprise quiz on verb tenses that she swore she never heard of let alone studied. She said she had to baby-sit her little sister last night while her parents went to dinner and bowling, and her sister is the devil's spawn.

I said I knew what she meant, not because I had a clue since I don't have any brothers or sisters and I never really study for anything, but it was better to let her talk, and then I didn't have to. Plus, I loved her accent with the last syllable of every sentence dragged out for about two minutes. She said her parents thought her sister was an angel, but the minute they were gone and she was in charge she was the devil. "Angel" was easily four syllables and "devil" had to have three. I should have asked her to say sugar to see if Kristen's aunt has it right.

Finally Bryan came. He was hurrying but didn't look happy.

"Something bad happened," he said as soon as he got

to us. "My dad was home when I got home from school. He had been laid-off, which he said was a polite way of saying he was fired. He had tried to shut down a boat line because there was some kind of bubbling in the gel coat, which I think is the outer, shiny layer.

"It was going to be real expensive to fix the equipment and the boats were no good according to my dad. At least, 'for that kind of money.' My dad is the meekest guy until he thinks he's absolutely right, and then he won't back down. He always says, 'Bryan, all you have is your integrity. When you are right, you have to stand your ground.' That's probably a good part of why we have moved so many times. The boss said they couldn't shut the line down, and my dad didn't back down. Now he's laid-off.

"I told him we can't move. I like this place. He told me he will try to get another job in town, but he can't promise anything because there really isn't a lot of industry. I thought he was going to cry. We have a one-year lease on our house and everything was going good, and he's so stubborn. It's always like this. Then he orders a big pizza with everything to make me feel better, but all I could think of was can we even afford it. Neither of us were hungry."

I didn't have a clue what to do or say. I thought Bryan was going to cry. Erin just took his hand in both of hers and said it would be all right. It was so easy for her. Why can't I do that?

We rushed out of the building and straight to her car. She had one of those old turquoise Pontiac Grand Ams. Go to any high school in America and you are going to see twenty per cent of the cars are Grand Ams in various states of entropy. You never see an adult drive one, but they all get passed down to kids somehow. Now that Pontiac is dead, what are kids supposed to do? Walk?

Hers had its share of rust and the plastic thing on the door was missing, but the interior was clean. Bryan offered to ride in the back, but I said I would when he was struggling with the whole seat sliding up two-door thing. He is all legs and it was tight back there for me. The shifter was on the floor and Erin shifted like it was a stick shift, which I didn't even know you could do.

It was only about five blocks to the city building and we didn't say a whole lot. I just kind of held on, cinching my shoulder harness tighter and tighter. She was one of those drivers who don't ever seem to look in front of them, adjusting the radio, the heat, her hair, anything until she was right on the bumper of the car in front, and somehow she knew to hit the brakes, hard. I swear we almost rear-ended three cars and each time she just giggled. Bryan was up front holding the grab bar above the window and just staring out the windshield.

When we got there and pulled safely into a space bumping the curb hard she said, "I never hit anyone." "Hit" had two syllables and Bryan and I sighed in unison.

"Ya'll know we can't just go in there and demand all the papers for the Little League park which shows that it's polluted, Erin said. "They'll know what we are doin'." The whole class had decided we should only go for the evidence on the park first. Just to try out the FOIA thing.

"I don't think we should tell them we are from the newspaper," Bryan said. "Maybe just tell them it's for a school report on the city parks."

"We can't do that. Mr. Dombrowski said we always have to identify ourselves as reporters."

"How about if we say our newspaper is doing a series of articles on city parks and this is the first one?"

"That has to work. That way we are identifying ourselves as reporters, and they'll be glad to give us the information. That okay with you, Lauren?" I nodded so we walked in. Bryan held the door for Erin and I seemed like an afterthought.

There was a lady at a desk with her back to us and she was sorting papers and filing them in folders and she didn't turn around to see us. I wondered if she was related to Mrs. Butt. We stood there, and stood there, and then I saw a bell that said, RING BELL FOR SERVICE. Bryan touched Erin's arm and pointed it out to her. She shook her head no, so just screwing around Bryan reached out like he was going to ring the bell and she grabbed his hand to stop him while whispering, "You'll scare her." Her hand stayed there way too long and he was obviously faking pushing the bell. I felt like I was in the back seat again, though this time the car was being driven by six-year-olds.

The lady finally asked, "May I help you?" Erin jerked back her hand.

Bryan said nothing so Erin stepped in. "We are doing a series of articles on the city parks for our high school newspaper and would like to FOIA some information on the Little League park since that one will be first."

"Oh that's no problem at all. You don't need a Freedom Form for that. That one is called, let me think, Riegle Park named after the president of KSR who donated it to the city." We wanted to file a FOIA. This was turning out so easy anyone could have done it. "Mr. Riegle actually donated two parks to the city. Let me see what I can find." She walked away behind some file cabinets with big plants hanging down. We could still see her head and I'm sure she could still hear us.

Erin elbowed Bryan. She was really physical. I

wanted to shout, "Hey, I'm here too." but I didn't.

"What are we going to do?" she whispered again to Bryan. "We're supposed to find out how the forms work."

"What if we just ask her?"

"She'll get suspicious."

"Apparently not if I ask. I'm innocent."

"Quiet. She's coming back. Try it." Erin was trying to suppress her giggles. She giggled easily.

"Here you are," the lady said. "That was easy. I made you a copy of the article with the ribbon cutting ceremony twenty, no twenty-one years ago. Sometimes I forget what year it is. And here's a copy of the deed and deed restrictions from KSR."

The elbow again. She got him right on the forearm. She must practice on her devil's spawn sister. "Thank you."

"You know I'm supposed to charge you a nickel a page for copies, but I'm not going to charge a school paper. That would be wrong. We always want to help good kids." Why were we good kids?

"We appreciate that," Erin said. "We have no budget at all." Then it just flowed like magic. From Erin.

"Would we all have had to pay if we had to file a Freedom Form?"

"Oh probably not. It says you do on the back. Here." She handed Bryan one. "You can keep that." She didn't wink, but it was almost as if she knew what we were after. I wondered if she was Colbert's source.

They said thank you again and goodbye. The lady asked me if she could help me, or if I was with them. I shook my head no, nodded toward them and hurried behind them to the car. I don't know exactly what we expected, but I felt like Julian Assange and Wikileaks back when he was still a good guy. Bryan started reading the Freedom Form out loud, and Erin was high-lighting the Little League papers. I was in the back wondering how it was so easy for most people to just talk. I guessed my mom really screwed me up. It had to be my mom.

"The law says they have to provide any and all paperwork on any subject we request as long as we properly fill out this form."

"Here's a picture of that Riegle guy and a bunch of others cutting a ribbon with a huge pair of scissors. Nothing else. Just the date and that KSR is donating the park for the benefit of our area youth."

I gave it a quick glance and saw nothing usable.

"They have up to five working days to provide the requested information."

"Oh this is better." Erin was really getting excited now. "In the deed restrictions, it says the city may not dig more than two foot deep for one-hundred years."

"It says that?" I said as I grabbed the paper. I guess I can talk if I get excited enough.

"We got them. Why else would they put that there unless they had something to hide?"

"Like hundreds of barrels of pollution." We high-fived as high as you could in a Grand Am.

"Anything else?"

"Just that should there be a major earthquake and barrels of toxic waste suddenly appear on the property, KSR makes no claim on them, and they are the sole responsibility of the city and all the city's taxpayers," Erin read from another page.

"It really says that?" Bryan asked.

"No dummy." And "Dummy" had four syllables and I was going to puke back there if she grabbed his hand again. I could picture myself in the back seat on their honeymoon silently telling everyone I was there when it all began. "Just that the city can't put a well or septic on the property."

"More evidence. Do you think it's enough to run a story?"

"It's suspicious, but it doesn't really prove anything."

"Mr. D. said we have to have two sources for any investigative article."

"I wonder if she gave us everything."

"I just had the feeling she was on our side, like Colbert's source. But it isn't likely that KSR gave the city any paperwork that tells how they polluted the land and then donated it for kids to play on."

"You're probably right. And I do think she was trying to help us. Don't you think, Lauren?" she turned and asked. I nodded. "Otherwise we never would have gotten that form."

"I was going to ask," Bryan said.

"You were going to sneak back in at night and climb in through the mail slot."

"Hey, Kevin got in trouble for that."

"Yeah, but he meant it in a mean way, and I said it in a nice way. Can't you tell the difference?"

I could tell. Bryan could tell. But I'm not going to go on telling you about the whole Erin and Bryan thing. She thought he looked like a runner, and he told her he eats and eats and eats and never gains any weight, and he was thinking about running cross-country this spring.

"Stop!" I almost had to yell. "If you guys want to hold hands, fall in love, go to the prom and have triplets, I don't care. Just not while I'm back here."

I could see they were embarrassed; we were all embarrassed. When I finally talk, why do I have to say such stupid things?

"We better get back to school," Erin said and threw the gear into reverse. It was quiet while she did the shift, shift, shift thing and Bryan and I hung on to whatever was near. She missed a lady in a crosswalk, but not by much.

When we got back to the school, they both turned to me and Bryan said we need to get ahold of that Miller guy who Randy talked about who hauled all the chemicals around so we can interview him. Erin said she was sorry for earlier. That made it worse.

Bryan's dad was waiting for him right outside the office. He was so excited because he had applied for unemployment and instead got a job. At KSR. It seems the guy in charge of Quality Control had a bad heart attack and his dad was a ready-made solution if only on a temporary basis until the guy recovered. He was real excited so none of us told him what we knew about KSR.

CHAPTER 15
SOYLENT GREEN

The January issue was a nightmare. We tried burning the whole paper on a disk and taking it directly to the newspaper, but it was all scrambled and unusable. So we used our old system of cutting and pasting, re-cutting and re-pasting. It was hard to get the energy to do it, because everyone was counting on the new system working. Even Matt couldn't figure it out. He just whispered curses on the computers, and Matt really isn't a cursing kind of guy. There was a lack of enthusiasm on that issue also, because it didn't have one article on KSR, and that is what we were all living and breathing. We decided not to print anything until we had it all, and it was slow.

So we covered the hockey team, Jennifer's hockey team. It was the boy's hockey team, but Jen wanted to play, and after a lot of nasty meetings with her parents and Silvers and the coach, they let her play. I don't think she was very good, but she took her shifts and always got back up off the boards. Some players let her skate almost unmolested, and others just used her as a straw man. Again, thank you Ms. Neihardt. She did get hit really hard once from behind, and her dad jumped over the wall and had to be restrained, but that was after we had published.

The Library was remodeled, big deal, and the first wind generator was going up south of town. Randy and Wayne wrote that and included a lot of pictures, big pictures, because we had to kill some space. I like the windmills.

Wayne tried to write a story on illegal immigration, but just about every businessperson he asked said they'd take their money no matter where it came from. Holly's dad even said he'd rent to Martians if they kept the house clean. JJ drew a cartoon of Mrs. Welch throwing loads of student papers into her fireplace for heat. Mrs. Welch retired last year. I guess that's how Dombrowski got his job. We all had her and she never graded papers. Never. We wrote them and turned them in knowing we'd never see them again. The cartoon was funny and it really kind of looked like her.

It wasn't until the following week that Bryan, Erin and I could go to see Mr. Miller. Randy had to get his name from his grandpa because there was a page and a half of Millers in the phone book, and Randy kept saying he forgot to ask. Mr. Dombrowski agreed that we needed more sources than our deed restrictions to prove the ball field was polluted, so we hoped Mr. Miller would be that next source.

Erin suggested we just drive to Mr. Miller's rather than phone him, because if he saw us in person maybe he could see that we were sincere. I think she wanted to get back in the car with Bryan because he still hadn't asked her out. Kristen told me, and she would know. I climbed right in the back, no questions. It kind of smelled this time, and I could see some pizza slice foils and crust remnants on the floor. So Erin really wasn't perfect.

We found the house right on the edge of the

industrial park. The park wasn't like you would picture. It had a few factories like the boatworks and KSR where we were before, a few houses like the Miller's which looked older and more run-down than the factories, a ball-field hiding barrels of toxic waste you couldn't see, and acres and acres of open fields with dead tall grasses.

Erin's driving hadn't improved, and when we drove into the Miller's driveway, which was all dirt and gravel, Bryan yelled stop and she did, which made a lot of noise. I couldn't see it from the back, but there was a bright yellow snowmobile parked in the driveway, and we ended up right against it. There was no damage because I don't think we ever really hit it.

"You don't need to yell, because I saw the snowmobile and was going to stop," Erin said.

"You are possibly the worse driver I've ever seen."

She made a face. "I've been driving for two years and never hit anything."

This stirred my heart, but mostly I wanted out.

Bryan said, "That's okay. There's no one he'd rather be in an accident with," which stirred my stomach.

That's when we noticed this guy standing not ten feet from us. The guy was way too young to be Mr. Miller. He couldn't have been more than thirty, so I thought Randy got us the wrong Miller. "Did you hit it?" he asked.

"No," Bryan said as he got out of the car. "I can still get a finger between the bumper and the sled. See." Bryan demonstrated it to the guy's satisfaction.

"Women drivers," the guy said but Bryan was smart enough not to have added anything.

"Are you Mr. Miller?" Erin asked.

"Yes."

"Tom Miller who worked at KSR?"

"Tommy, yes. But that was my dad at KSR. Why?"

Bryan jumped in. "We're from the high school paper and want to interview him."

"About what?"

"About KSR. What he did there and stuff."

Erin asked, "Does he still live here? Can we talk to him?"

This guy just seemed suspicious, and it wasn't the way I pictured this interview working. I wondered if he was mad about the snowmobile. And there was no snow.

"He doesn't live here anymore."

"Can you tell us where he lives so we can ask him some questions?"

"No I can't. He's dead. Two years."

Erin said she was sorry to hear that, which is what you are supposed to say, even though she never even met the man. I was sorry because we couldn't get the answers we needed, and this son was looking like a jerk who wasn't going to help us.

"What did you want to ask him?"

I wanted to leave. Tommy made me uncomfortable. He wasn't taller than Bryan, just bigger. Way bigger. My mom always said girls are better at judging people than guys, and anytime I am uncomfortable, leave. I think Erin felt the same because she pulled on Bryan's arm to get him to go, but instead he told Tommy the truth. "We're trying to find out if KSR polluted this industrial park, and we think your dad would know."

"Hell yes they did. And not just this park. All over town. And now you ought to see what those bastards are trying to do to my momma." He seemed to like his momma much more than I liked mine.

"What are they trying to do to her?" Bryan asked.

"They're trying to take away her house. She's sixty-three and lived here since she and Daddy married and now they want to tax us right out of our house to clean up their mess. That bastard Riegle always told him, 'Just do your job and dump the stuff and we'll take care of you.' Take care of us by dumping a sixty-three-year-old lady out of the only decent house she's ever had. What is she supposed to do? She used to work at K-Mart, but they're gone and she could never pay for a house on that. I'm doing everything I can, but you can't buy a house in this town with the wages they pay. Are you going to help?"

"How can we help?" Bryan asked. I thought he meant help buy them a new house.

"Print it in your paper. Tell the town what KSR done and is trying to do to Momma. I've been to the newspaper and the television and none of those bastards will do anything." He obviously liked the word bastard.

"I don't know what we can do. We're not afraid to print the truth, but we need evidence," Bryan said. I was surprised by how much better he was with this half-crazy guy than he was with the lady at the city.

"I'll give you evidence. Let's go talk to Momma." He led us straight up the driveway and into the house where his mother apparently still lived. "Ma," he shouted loud enough so some of the factory workers a block away running presses and welders and really noisy machines must have stopped work and looked around.

His mom came in and she didn't look all that old, but I guessed she was pretty deaf. "These kids want to write a story about Dad and how they are trying to take away our house." He was still loud and we didn't really know anything about someone taking away their house other than the little bit we heard from Tommy. I was still uncomfortable.

"Oh, God bless you children." I thought that was nice. She stared straight into my eyes, and it was like she grabbed on and had no intention of letting go. She didn't talk loud at all. In fact, you had to listen quietly or you'd miss what she said.

"My Tom was a good man. He just did what he was told."

I was excited. I mean we were really doing it, getting real evidence, bringing down the bad guys. "Are you really going to tell our story? No one else will."

"We intend to," Erin said way too loud. Mrs. Miller seemed to be talking to me looking between the other two since she was still staring at my eyes every time I looked at her, although I didn't look all that often.

"You don't need to shout," even though it was Erin who had shouted. "I can hear you just fine. Tommy just thinks I'm deaf because I ignore him most of the time, and I turn the TV on high. I guess I ignore that most of the time too. I miss my Tom."

"We are trying to write a story on KSR. We think they polluted Shadyside and maybe a bunch of other places in town. We don't really know anything about someone trying to take away your home, but if that's true, we'll write about that too." Erin answered much quieter now, and Mrs. Miller looked at her seeming to hear just fine. I thought, first Mrs. Fortuni and now this. Why are the crazy ladies attracted to me?

"It's all true. Everything out here is polluted and Tom had a lot to do with it, although he was only doing what he was told to do. Warren Riegle told Tom, 'You just do as I say and I'll take care of everything.' Tom always liked Warren. I'll bet if Tom's looking down on us now he'd like to be spitting wads of chew on Warren. Tom liked his chew. I think that's probably what killed him. Cancer. I hated the chew, but Tom was a good man, a good provider for all of us."

"What was his job?" Bryan asked. I looked at Bryan and he was smiling at her, but when I looked back, Mrs. Miller was back staring at me. I began to wonder if she ever blinked. Wouldn't that make a great *WaterGate Post* headline, BODIES OF THREE MISSING STUDENTS DISCOVERED UNDER THE FLOORBOARDS OF AREA HOME. Tommy was staring at Bryan.

"He was kind of Warren's gopher. You know. Someone who has to go for everything. At least once a week he had to get rid of the waste. They had lots of waste there. Sometimes it would take Tom three trips to the dump to haul it all. But usually just one. We used to have a big old dump truck. Actually, I guess it was KSR's, but Tom took it home every weekend and made money on the side. We'd save that extra money up and go to Florida once a year. The whole family. Even the grandkids. We have six now. The last time we went we had four, so all nine of us went. Disney World and everything. I've got pictures." She looked away from me and pointed to a picture on an old buffet with kids, and Mickey, and Tommy who was much younger then.

"What kind of waste and where did he haul it?" Bryan asked. I suspected she would get around to telling us but couldn't be rushed.

"Just junk from the factory. Not metals or anything. Chemicals. They used to just use floor drains and it ran out back, but they got in some kind of trouble and started putting the stuff in barrels. Tom had to get rid of the barrels. Usually he took them to the dump, but sometimes he dumped them in the swamp by the airfield or the swamp by the Sheriff's office. Some were supposed to be incinerated, but I think those were mostly the ones Tom put in the swamp."

Erin asked, "Did he ever dump them where the Little League park is now?"

"Heavens yes, dear." Bingo. "That was once a swamp too. Sometimes he just dumped the chemicals and sometimes it was whole barrels. He just did what he was told."

"Not all the time, Ma," Tommy broke in.

"See, a few times he didn't make it to the dump on time on Fridays so he would just dump the barrels out back if he had a weekend load for the truck." She pointed towards their backyard, which I could see through the window, but I couldn't see any barrels from where I was sitting. "Tom was always going to move those barrels but he never got around to it."

"They never leaked," Tommy rapidly interjected. "We played on them all the time when we were kids." Some dad.

"Well the city said they did and now they want us to pay, even though KSR already paid to haul them away just after Tom passed on."

"That's why we might lose the house," Tommy said.

"If they're gone, how can the city charge you?" Bryan asked.

"Because they're bastards," Tommy said and he really emphasized the "bastards" part making them sound truly evil.

"Tommy, you watch your language in my house," Mrs. Miller said and she finally looked away from me to glance briefly at the crucifix off to my right. But it was back to me when she said, "The city said the barrels leaked and contaminated the groundwater and we have to pay our share to clean it up."

That really didn't seem all that unfair to me. Who in their right mind would bring barrels of chemicals home and let their children play on them. Modify headline.

MISSING STUDENTS FOUND IN BARRELS IN AREA HOME'S BACKYARD. Erin asked, "What do they consider your fair share?"

"Don't you ever say anything?" she asked me.

"Not much," I said and I tried to unlock her eye contact. "What is your fair share according to the city." I felt really involved.

"The last notice the city gave us said we could be charged twenty thousand dollars."

"Just for a few barrels?" Bryan really sounded amazed.

"That's every year!"

"Every year! For how long?" I truly was amazed both at the twenty thousand dollars and my talking.

"They don't know. They are guessing it will be at least forty years, but probably longer. They don't just want us to pay for any pollution from our yard; they want everyone to pay for all of KSR's pollution."

Erin asked, "What happens if you don't pay?"

"What do you mean if?" she asked. "There is no if. There's no money here. I'm still trying to pay off some of Tom's medical bills the insurance didn't cover. When we fall two years behind, we lose the house, and it's not worth three year's taxes."

"That's so unfair," Bryan said under his breath.

Tommy added, "It's all KSR. Riegle told Dad not to worry. He would take care of us and now he's the one charging us to clean his mess."

Bryan said, "I thought it was the city who was charging you twenty thousand a year."

"It is," Mrs. Miller said. "But it is Warren who is making them do it. The EPA came in after the DNR did a bunch of test wells and ordered KSR to clean up all the barrels and groundwater. They took KSR to court and KSR lost. Lost big." I remembered Colbert saying something about that. "That will cost millions and millions. So KSR is saying everyone contributed to the pollution, so everyone benefits by the clean-up, so everyone needs to pay. So, the city is looking at a special assessment tax to make everyone pay, not just KSR."

"Why would the city do that Mrs. Miller?" Erin asked.

Then she made us start calling her Doris, which is my grandma's name on my dad's side. My mom never wants me to call adults by their first name "Warren. He has all kinds of big political friends and look at all the jobs KSR provides. One threat from him to move the jobs down south or to Mexico or even worse, to China, and he gets whatever he wants."

"Have you tried talking to him since he said he would take care of you?" Bryan asked.

"That Bastard, sorry Ma," Tommy said really spitting it this time. "He won't return our calls and I sat outside his office until he had security come lead me away. I felt like punching one of them and then running out the door, but it wouldn't do any good unless I could punch Riegle. We'll never see him and Ma used to bake him cookies."

"They were just chocolate chip but he seemed to like them. He was different then." I knew we had to include the cookie thing in our final story. Mr. Dombrowski would love it.

"So Doris," I said since she was looking at me and Tommy was creeping me out. "How can we help?"

"You've got to let people know what they're doing to us."

Right away I thought of *Grapes of Wrath* with Rosasharn's, who I couldn't stand, baby in the basket, but Bryan did something really stupid. He said, "Soylent Green is people" which is a line from this old

B grade movie we watched in Mr. Knudson's government class. Mr. Knudson pronounces his name Ka-nood-son and on the first day Kristen told him and the whole class she 'ca-ouldn't wait to get to ka-no all the ka-noledge that Mr. Ka-noodson was going to teach us,' and she thanked him and sat down. I wish I had her guts. I started remembering the ending of the movie and the scoops, which were really garbage trucks, even though the movie wasn't actually funny at all, but it fit so perfectly, and then Bryan and Erin giggled back, which made us look stupid and unprofessional.

Doris almost looked peeved. Yes, she was still staring at me. Then Tommy burst in, "That's my favorite flick. It's people. Soylent Green is people," and his voice died off like he was choking. I kind of pictured him more like a *Deliverance* or Freddie kind of guy which was even worse than *Soylent Green,* but I watched *Deliverance* with my dad. Tommy fell to the floor saying, "It's people….people," and I was grateful Bryan didn't join him in a male bonding Soylent ritual.

It had to be difficult ignoring Tommy on the floor, but Erin said, "You gave us just what we needed to run a story on the Little League park. We've already got two other students working on the federal lawsuit against KSR, but we didn't know anything about this tax thing."

"Special assessment," Tommy said still from the floor, and I wondered what could be wrong with a thirty-year old guy rolling on the floor. No wonder he still lived with his momma.

"We'll try to find out more about that if we can, and write about it too if we can get the evidence," Erin said. "But our teacher makes us get at least two sources for everything and we only print one paper a month, so it will take time."

"I have one more question," Bryan said. "Do you know what kind of chemicals were in the barrels and dumped on the ground?"

"Oh, no, dear. I'm not even sure Tom knew most of the time. It was just his job, and he did it," Doris said and finally made eye contact with Bryan. I wondered if she would latch onto him like she did me, but then she turned back to me and I had to look away.

"The city sent you a list, Ma," Tommy said finally sitting up again but still from the floor. "They said they were degreasers and coolants and Chromium. Chromium was the real bad one."

"I threw that away I was so mad."

"Does that sound like the stuff your husband handled?" Bryan asked. I was really impressed.

"That sounds about right. Would you children like to stay for lunch? I can make macaroni and cheese. My grandchildren love it."

Erin said, "No we can't. We have another class." And I looked at my watch and discovered that next class was almost half over.

"We have to go!" I said to Bryan while pointing at my watch. I was hoping I wouldn't have to step over Tommy to get away.

"Can we call you if we have any more questions?" Bryan asked as we headed for the door.

"Of course dear. Of course. Just send us one of your papers when you are done."

"And get that Bas..." but he stopped. "Riegle," he finished.

She shook Erin's hand and then mine, which was a little weird but nothing like Tommy. He grabbed Bryan by the ankle. "It's people. You gotta tell them. Soylent Green is people." When Bryan got his leg free he was the first one out the door, barely holding it for us. I didn't blame him.

Believe me. Erin was careful to put the car in reverse and not run over the snowmobile. She pulled into the Little League park so we could figure out what to do next. From the back seat I said, "That was weird."

Erin grabbed Bryan's leg. "It's people," in a real low voice. And he grabbed her's saying, "Soylent Green is people."

They giggled a lot. I didn't feel like playing Soylent Green.

"We won't make it back to school until lunch," Erin said. "We might as well go to Burger King."

They both turned and asked me if that was all right, and I said I didn't care. What a thrill. I got to be there on their first date. Chaperone. They ate from the dollar menu and I had a Whopper Meal Deal, which sounded better than it was, and I could scarcely eat all the fries. I wrote about it in my next column.

Bryan got into trouble because both of them missed Knudson's class and there was a quiz. Erin's mom excused her, but Bryan's dad wouldn't write him an excuse, so he had to take a zero. He didn't want to tell his dad how important the interview was because then he would have to tell him all about KSR. And he sure wasn't going to tell him about Erin.

CHAPTER 16
BRYANANDERIN

Kristen just called them BryananderiN, all one word. We don't mind a couple, but this is high school and they had to do everything together. They walked together; waited outside each other's classrooms; ate together in the cafeteria. It about made Kristen and me want to puke together. Kristen guessed Erin was after him right after that Abou butt thing. And the paper made Abou too. She dated a mess of guys right after the picture, but then she steadied with Danny Harper, the starting center on our basketball team, and he's a year younger than her and at least a foot taller. High school. I'm so glad it's over.

BryananderiN did set the standard though. They got KSR. They wrote the story, which I was supposed to help on, but mysteriously was finished when I wasn't around. They did put my name on it, third again, and I supposed I did edit it. Everyone loved it. Dombrowski loved it. They had two good sources to show Riegle Park was polluted by KSR. Plus Doris Miller was a sympathetic character, almost as much as Mrs. Fortuni, 'Lauren's crazy lady' as everyone refers to Kristen's aunt's neighbor. And so far I hadn't found anything solid enough to back up her story. Doris used to bake

Riegle cookies, and now she was going to lose her home. Compare that to my lady losing her husband who she loved dearly to cancer. I win. I guess it isn't a competition, but in some ways it is, and I felt left out on the BryananderiN Miller story.

Kristen and I decided to research the special assessment story, and how KSR wasn't planning on paying for the clean-up. That was a whole lot harder than just knocking on someone's door and asking a few questions.

Now what if we were lesbians, Kristen and I? I mean we're not, though she once told me she kissed a girl but I think that was another one of her 'let me see Lauren's face turn red' stories. Nobody questioned when Kristen and I went to the city hall on the following Monday. No third person had to go with us. Front seat for me. Driving. Political correctness involves a lack of trust.

We had to talk to the same lady BryananderiN and I saw before, so I put on my Redsox baseball cap and made a ponytail through the adjustable strap so the lady wouldn't recognize me. Kristen thought I was being paranoid, that there was no way she was going to recognize me and what difference would it make.

I must have looked hurt because she then said, "Lauren, if you don't talk to people, they don't see you. Besides she's a lady. If she were a young stud boy, then she'd remember you." She smiled. I smiled. We walked in.

The lady who was so friendly last time wasn't friendly at all. When Kristen asked for the papers for the special assessment, she just stared at us and said, "What special assessment?" and we didn't know. I felt like an idiot because I thought she would just give us whatever we needed.

Kristen said, "The one involving KSR," which I

thought was good.

But the lady said, "Which one?" We didn't have a clue. How could we know there was more than one?

"The one involving their polluting the water in the industrial park and Shadyside subdivision," Kristen tried. That seemed to work.

"You'll have to fill out a Freedom Form. Here," she said handing us a form.

So Kristen and I sat down at a little table to fill out the form. We used my name and address because I lived in the city, and where it said *specific information you are requesting:* we wrote in just what Kristen said, "all special assessment papers involving KSR's polluting the water in the industrial park and Shadyside subdivision." I signed it and we brought it back up to the lady.

She took it, glanced at it, and didn't say anything. We stood there and waited for her to bring us back the papers and she didn't move. Finally, she said, "Is there anything else I can help you with?"

Kristen said, "When will we get the papers?" She said it real nice the way only Kristen can when she doesn't like someone.

But the lady said kind of snappily, "We have five working days and then we'll mail it to you along with a bill. Didn't you read the back?"

"Yes, ma'am. Thank you for all your help." Kristen sounded so sincere I would have fallen for it if I didn't know her so well.

When we got outside Kristen said, "I thought you said she was nice and would just give us the papers."

"She was when I was here with Bryan and Erin."

"Maybe she got in trouble for the papers she gave you last time." I drove straight back to school. No Burger King.

"Do you want to go to Carol's Cookies?"

"I'm not in the mood."

While we were waiting for the evidence, Kevin contacted the EPA whose nearest office was on the other side of the state and requested a transcript of the suit against KSR. They told him, "You have to purchase it through a third party, a reporting company near the state capitol."

He thought at first maybe another newspaper was going to trump our story, but he figured out they must be court reporters. So Kevin contacted them.

"We can have it for you in about two weeks," they said, "unless there's a rush."

"We're kind of in a hurry," Kevin said.

"It's four dollars a page, plus postage for the rush order, and you can have it in two days."

"How many pages are there," Kevin asked.

"It was a big trial. I estimate it's ten thousand pages, including evidence."

Kevin almost dropped the phone. It took us more than a month to raise the money to test the water in the school. Nobody can drink that much pop.

Kevin asked, "How much for the two-week version?"

"Two dollars a page."

"I'll get back to you." Kevin hung up.

When he reported it back to the class we didn't know how we were ever going to get those papers and they seemed to be the key. Kristen and I reported that it was now the fifth day and we still hadn't heard back from the city so we were expecting our papers on Monday. It was a slow, frustrating week. Nothing had broken since BryananderiN's story. We kept working on March's edition, but our heart still wasn't in it. We weren't going to print any articles about the water pollution thing until we had all the stories, and that was where all the effort was going. Kristen and I went back to Shadyside and talked to four more neighbors, but none of them knew as much as our "crazy lady" or us.

Monday, when I got home from school, I went straight for the mail and there it was, a letter from the city. But it was a lot smaller than I anticipated. I opened it up and it was a form letter that said our Freedom Form was rejected. They had a lot of little check boxes at the bottom and the one marked: *insufficient information*, was checked. I didn't even know what that meant. Kristen was going to be steamed. That lady could have told us right there that we had insufficient information if she had wanted to. In fact, when I called Kristen the first thing she did was refer to her as the bitch -lady.

On Tuesday, we reported our news to the class.

Sean suggested, "Maybe since we didn't really have anything going in the March edition, we can just run a headline such as: CITY BREAKS FEDERAL LAW AND REFUSES FOIA. We can use one hundred font and dump that stupid story on the Carnegie Library in town and how it is falling apart. Everyone already knows that."

"Hey, that's my stupid Carnegie story!" both Randy and Amy yelled almost in unison.

I think they hated each other by this time in the year. I don't know how they got stuck together, but I guess it was probably because the rest of us were working so hard on KSR. Sean had to back down because Randy is intimidating, and Amy is a female. I don't think he meant anything by it anyway. It was just his way of expressing his frustration at the city, the difficulty finding hard evidence, and the conservative nature of the newspaper since we were always getting into trouble with Silvers.

I like Sean's demeanor. He'd be all right if he

weren't constantly leering at the girls and then looking away and innocent when he got caught. Maybe we did need to attack the city, but he shouldn't have dissed the Carnegie story. The article on the library was good. People need to pay attention to old buildings.

When it looked like the whole class was going to break up into backstabbing seventh-graders, Matt spoke up. He speaks second least. Obviously, I'm number one. It's good to be number one for something.

"I'm sure I can hack into the city's computer and get whatever information you need." He didn't even bother to look up from the computer he was dismantling. We had run an ad in our last paper asking for donations of unwanted computers and received three, though Matt said they really weren't capable of running our software but could be recycled for parts. The school's computer gods wanted nothing to do with them, or Matt, since whenever they came to look at one of our computers, Matt had to patiently explain what was wrong and what we needed. Mr. D. only called them when Matt needed parts.

The kids right away jumped all over Matt's idea until Mr. Dombrowski ended it by saying, "Matt, Matt, Matt. This is Obi One Kenobi, Matt. Turn from the dark side. Princess Leia is waiting for you."

I don't know or care if I spelled Obi One Kenobi's name right. A bunch of us tried telling Mr. Dombrowski that Star Wars stuff was way uncool and it didn't faze him. Sean said maybe he should stick to his lame Shakespeare renditions and most of us agreed we liked those better than Star Wars.

But Matt said, "Is Princess Leia getting here anytime soon, Mr. Dombrowski?"

"The right girl for you is just one galaxy away and kicking it in to Warp Speed, Matt."

"Thanks, Mr. Dombrowski," and Matt turned his attention back to the computer.

They had kind of a weird relationship, but I think Matt really grew in that class. I even thought about going out on a date with him. He was sort of cute, smart, and definitely nice, but he was so desperate, and if I went out with him everyone would think I was desperate, and I am not desperate. And I wouldn't have a clue how to ask him. And that would be a heck of a date, two and a half hours of silence and then, "Did you like the movie?" "Uh huh, you?" "Yeah."

As Mr. Dombrowski lectured the class on all the reasons why we can't use "purloined" evidence (he always liked to use words like that to expand our vocabulary), I thought he must be getting a bit desperate by now. He'd been in Grandma's house for five months now, and I'd never seen him with a date. He did disappear for just about the whole two week Christmas break, but I know he took stacks of papers with him that needed correcting and he passed back a mess of them to all his classes on the first day back. None of his mail ever looked like love letters, but I couldn't tell you about Saturday's or holiday's. Maybe that's why he could understand Matt.

Colbert was saying maybe he could help get the information, and I began to think we were never going to get out of there. Finally Kristen said, "We have to go" and Mr. Dombrowski said, "Go" so we went.

Kristen drove because she drives faster. The lady at the City Hall was still behind the counter, and she was helping an old lady who wanted to know why her tax bill was three dollars and seven cents higher than last year's. The city lady looked at us and I could feel a chill of recognition. It was almost as if she spent a lot more time with the old lady than she had to. Kristen said afterwards she was ready to just give the old lady three dollars and seven cents.

"May I help you?" she asked as the old lady walked away. I held the door because I really didn't want to be next to Kristen when she blew.

I expected Kristen to smack the letter flat on the counter waking up all the backroom dozing bureaucrats and demanding to know what the meaning of this was and where are our damn papers were, but she was sweet. "We don't understand this letter and we need your help," she said. I almost let the door go on the old lady.

"Well let me see," she said and took the letter. She pointed to the checkmark near *insufficient information* and said, "Oh see. You have insufficient information."

"Yes, I saw your check-mark, but I don't know what that means."

"Well that's easy. It means you didn't have enough information." Here she returned Kristen's smile and I just knew that was a mistake.

"I know what insufficient means and just about any word you or any…" and she stopped and reverted back to her smiling. "We need to know how to get sufficient information."

"Just properly fill out the form and we'll mail it to you in five business days." Kristen waved me up to come closer and I inched up almost alongside of her. "You see my friend Lauren here?"

"Yes."

"Well, she's practically deaf and dumb and not very smart either." The lady looked at me and nodded as if it were obvious. "Now this was her form, and she did her very best, but obviously made some kind of a mistake. Can you help her get the information she needs?"

"Can she hear me at all?" This was really

embarrassing, but we were too far into this for me to ruin it.

"She can read your lips if you look right at her."

"Okay," she said to me. I went a little further behind Kristen. "If you write down what you want, we can get it for you."

"She did that once," Kristen said.

"But it was insufficient."

"Let's not go there again. You know what documents my friend Lauren is after. Now what does she have to write on the line to get those documents?"

She whispered to Kristen, "Mr. Walker says she has to write down the exact names of the documents she wants or it is insufficient."

"Who is Mr. Walker, and how is my friend Lauren supposed to know the names of the documents she needs if she has never seen them?"

"He is the city manager, my boss." Then she whispered again, "No matter what your friend does, if she doesn't have the exact names, she will never see those documents." Then to me she said, "Good Luck."

I said, "Thank you," and she turned to Kristen and said, "She talks very well."

Kristen said, "We're working on it."

I about smacked Kristen when we got back to the car. "Why did you call me deaf and dumb?"

"It almost worked. I think she wanted to help a dumb person."

"How are we ever going to get the documents?"

"We've got to find the names, but I don't know how?"

"I thought you were going to give her hell."

"Maybe next time."

CHAPTER 17
FREE AT LAST

The next time came the next day. Colbert came running and stumbling up to Kristen and me the following morning, because Colbert doesn't actually run. He's just not smooth—smart, but not smooth. Kristen said she thought 'oh not this again,' because Colbert had asked her out not three weeks before. She had just broken up with her boyfriend of the month, if you can call him that. They had dated since Christmas, so more than a month. He took it hard and it was all over school, so Colbert knew just like everyone else. Colbert cornered her after class and she never saw it coming, him asking her out.

She was actually kind of excited. Usually I just hear about them like everyone else, but she told me about Colbert. In fact, she told Dombrowski too. She didn't think she was too good for him; if anything, he was too good for her. He wanted to save the world, and she was still trying to find her place in it. She realized that to start dating people like Colbert, she'd have to become a better person and decided she wasn't ready for that. She told him she wasn't ready to begin dating so soon after the last boyfriend, and he seemed to accept it.

"Kristen, I got it! Kristen I got it!" Like I wasn't

there. He kept saying it and he wasn't even near us yet. I'm thinking the dating thing so I'm wondering: tickets, a condom, a speaking engagement at the Democratic convention, herpes? He showed her a paper, which I saw said something about special assessments, but I didn't know what. He was grinning and if he had been wearing his little bow tie I bet it would have been spinning little beanie cap circles.

Kristen said, 'Slow down, Colbert. What is this?"

"That's what you need. For the city. My secret source said that's it. You write those names on the form and they have to give them to you." She handed it to me and there were three names: Special Assessment 24, KSR Draft A, Special Assessment 24, KSR Draft B, Special Assessment 24, KSR Draft C.

Kristen grabbed him and kissed him on the cheek right in the high school cafeteria which was probably a mistake. Catatonic was not a good look for him. Kristen said, "Colbert. It was just a kiss. A thank you. Don't take it as any more than that, okay?"

"Okay," but it was a mousy little okay. I could see it was the best day of his life.

"You're sure these will work?"

"They'll work. But you can't tell them you got them from me."

"I won't. But if they get us the papers, I am going to tell the class where we got the names." He just grinned and we ran to tell Dombrowski we were going straight to city hall instead of to class today.

Kristen asked the lady for another Freedom Form for her friend, and she handed one to me.

I said, "Thank you very much," and Kristen said to the lady, "See, we're still working on it."

We filled out the form exactly as Colbert wrote it, and we wondered if we could put all three requests on the same form or if they had to be separate. We only had one form so that's what we did, and then we marched straight up to the lady and placed it gently on the counter like we did this every day.

She looked it over carefully, then stared straight at me. "Where did you get these?"

I had kind of crept behind Kristen, so she asked me if I wanted to handle this. I pretended to read her lips and shook my head no.

Kristen looked at the lady. "You told us yesterday to be sufficient we need to write down the exact names so there they are. May we have the documents now, please."

I smiled at her but she probably never saw it. She left us standing at the counter until she came back two minutes later with this short guy wearing a blue suit and a power red tie. His hair was slicked back very New York, but it didn't work in small town America.

"Where did you get this?" he wanted to know. His voice didn't fit his frame and it wasn't like he was going to intimidate Kristen.

"Hi. My name's Kristen and this is my friend Lauren." She reached out to shake his hand. I didn't reach out anything. The power tie worked.

"I'm Mr. Walker, City Manager." He did shake Kristen's hand but didn't know how to deal with me since he would have had to kick his belly up onto the counter to get his hand anywhere near me. He nodded. "Which one of you is Lauren?"

I didn't move, which was probably a good thing because the lady pointed to me and told Mr. Walker I was deaf and dumb.

"OK then," he said looking at Kristen and ignoring me completely. "Now where did you get these names?"

"Why? That is not a part of the form?" Kristen said.

"We are curious."

"Mr. Walker, I cannot tell a lie," Kristen lied. "I am somewhat of a visionary. After your clerk here yesterday helpfully suggested to us that in order not to have insufficient information we needed the exact names of the documents, I went straight to work. I got the first one right away, but the second and third took me most of the night. I'm a little sleepy today."

His face started to match his tie. "Okay then, who sent you and what do you want the information for?"

"Mr. Walker," Kristen said. "Did we properly fill out the form?"

"It appears that you have. Are you going to answer my questions?"

"Your questions are personal and have nothing to do with the Freedom of Information Act, so probably not."

"Okay. We are very busy here and it will take some time to fill your request." He turned and walked away, and he was cursing but I couldn't catch the words.

Then we began our second wait for the city's secret deal.

While waiting, Kevin had an epiphany.

CHAPTER 18
CUTE DNR GUY

Okay, so Kevin didn't have an epiphany. I know that everyone who is in this book will get a copy and will recognize themselves, pseudonyms and all. Some will still like me and some won't, and I'm okay with that. It was high school. But Sean, when you read that line, I knew it would stroke you out and that's what you get for trying to look down all the girl's shirts and saying the things you said.

Kevin took the credit for Sean's idea, and Sean told everyone that Kevin hasn't had an epiphany since he discovered he could see himself in his Jell-O. Kevin is a nice guy and all, and he really has an artistic talent that I could almost be jealous of, but he is not going to discover the next planet. He did do a lot of complaining and moaning about how he was supposed to get the documents from the court reporter and they were going to cost twenty thousand dollars, forty if we want them fast. But he didn't do anything about it.

After three or four days of this Sean told him, "Listen, your old man is rich. Instead of whining like a little girl why don't you just buy them? It must be some kind of a tax write off."

It's true. This kid has a summer car and a winter car.

And they're his. I know when he was in elementary and his dog died, he was so upset his parents had it stuffed for him. It was a standard poodle, black. I saw it at his birthday party. Who has room for that to hang around a house? He does. If it's still there, how can he bring a date home? He'd say, 'Hey you want to pet my dog?' and she'd pee her pants. Kevin whipped Sean the secret finger guys do to each other when the teacher's back is turned.

Kevin said, "If you're so freaking smart like you always say you are, you get the freaking papers." Too many freakings.

"Is there any place else to get the papers?"

"For forty thousand they'll rush them."

"I know. You've been saying that all week. Who else was involved in the trial?"

"KSR of course but they're not going to give it to us."

"You're doing good, boy." Sean laughed, and Kevin slid out another finger by straightening his glasses.

"So I guess we are SOL unless you trip over a stack of them while you are walking home after school. Walking. Walking. Walking."

Sean looked around the room, I'm sure hoping no one heard the walking part because everyone knew his parents took his car away for bad grades at the semester.

He stopped at Erin and stared, rude even for Sean. "Erin," he called. "Didn't that the Miller lady say the DNR drilled the wells for the EPA?"

"Yeah."

He turned back to Kevin. "And don't we have a DNR office right in town, and they are a government bureaucracy, and what is the one thing bureaucracies love more than anything else?" Pause for an answer that he knew was never going to come. "Paper. They probably have copies of everything we need. We just need to figure out how to get them out of there."

Sean and Kevin became a team. It sounded like a good match. Sean's brains, Kevin's respectable good looks and his cool car. I figured no one would give the information to Sean, but Kevin, if he didn't say anything too stupid, had a chance. I shouldn't be so hard on Sean, but I once overheard him telling Kevin that he should ask me out.

"Lauren is your best option since Erin is taken by that wuss Bryan, and frankly, you'll never make Kristen. You could take Lauren to a movie. You'd look good. She'd look a hell of a lot better. You'd say, ,How did you like the movie?' She'd grunt. You'd say something funny. She'd grunt twice. You'd say, 'Do you want to make out?' She'd slap you clear to Rite-Aid."

I was right there and he had to know I was listening. Parts of it hurt, but I didn't mind being third to Kristen and Erin.

The next school day, Monday, went bad for me. Kevin and Sean were to go to the DNR, but Sean had no car and Kevin's Ram was in for its twelve thousand mile checkup. They needed a ride and they asked me. I looked for Kristen who wasn't nearby, and she just shook her head no so I said no. They asked the whole class and everyone had an excuse. They asked me again and I shook my head no.

Mr. D. got involved and everyone stuck to their cheap excuses so that they didn't have to be in the same car as Sean. So he apologized and asked me, offering me one million and one extra credit points, because we really needed the information. I gave in but told him I needed to use at least two hundred thousand for English. He thanked me. He wasn't too tough to talk to.

So the three of us again, me driving, went to the

DNR. Since this was my third time doing something like this, I spoke. There were two guys there and they spoke more to me anyway, and the young guy was cute. I told them we wanted copies of any evidence concerning the groundwater pollution caused by KSR. They made us sign in and took us to a sitting room. I thought, wow I'm good, but I learned later they have to do this.

The young guy delivered three huge boxes, just like that. They were each about the size you see kids peddling free kittens in front of supermarkets and they were overloaded. It was funny because he brought each one in separately on a cart.

"Read everything," he said. Mark anything you want with sticky notes, and we will copy them for five cents a page."

Sean asked Mr. Big spender, "Can you afford five cents a page since you didn't have to drive your big five mpg Ram to school today?"

Another finger, but we were almost giddy with all the information.

The guy who wheeled them in stayed with the third box and started talking to us.

"Why do you want the information?"

I wondered if we should tell him.

Kevin said "school."

"What for in school?"

We looked at each other and Kevin did well, not talking.

The guy said, "Look guys, it will take you at least a month to really go through those boxes. If I know what you are looking for, I can save you a hell of a lot of time."

I actually thought the "hell" was good. I thought he put it in there to show us he was cool and could be trusted.

Sean told him, "We are trying to do a newspaper article for the school paper."

"Can you be more specific?"

"We could," Sean said. "But we don't know if that is smart. Nobody seems to want us to have the information."

"Try this," he said. "I'm going to make a guess based on your request and if I am right you can stomp your left foot two times. If I am wrong you can ignore me and have at the boxes."

Sean nodded, but I thought, "Is this guy fooling around for me, or do we really need to be that secretive?"

"I'm going to guess you think KSR polluted the hell out of the industrial park and now they don't want to pay to clean it up."

"Are we right?" Kevin asked all excited.

"You didn't stomp your foot." So Kevin stomped his left foot two times. I told you he was a moron.

"We are right aren't we?" I said.

"Mostly," he answered. "KSR wasn't the only one. They just did most of it, and like any decent stockholder-fearing corporation, don't want to pay for any of the clean-up."

"And we can prove that all right here."

"It's all there. But if I were you, I'd start with the Federal Judge's order. It summarizes thousands of pages of testimony. In fact, the trial was never actually completed. The case against KSR was so strong, the judge issued a summary judgment ordering KSR to immediately begin clean-up. However, that was almost two years ago."

"So this has already been in the papers?" I asked, feeling like all we were doing was reprinting old news.

"No. Not in the local newspaper. We sent them

releases and sections of the order just like we would in any big case, but they never printed any of it. Do you know who Warren Riegle is?"

By this time he was digging through one of the boxes until he came up with what looked like a four page document.

"He was CEO of KSR and his name keeps coming up everywhere," Sean said.

"He is connected. I have no doubt he can keep anything he wants out of our local rag. Hell, we couldn't touch him until we changed governors and now we're back there again if you know what I mean."

"Colbert would appreciate that," Sean said.

"Colbert is his name?"

"No, it's Daryl. But he hates all Republicans, so he calls himself Colbert after Colbert on Comedy Central." He stretched out the second one like Colbearrrrrr.

"This is normal?" he asked me.

"It seems to be in our high school."

"Okay then. This will get you most of what you need," he said handing Kevin the document. "I'm going to be about three cubicles that way in the next room if you need anything at all. Good luck."

Kevin handled the document as if it were the missing gospels to the New Testament. Sean took it from Kevin and sat on the padded bench near the window. Kevin and I had no choice but to sit on either side. It was called: KSR/Possum Plating vs. Environmental Protection Agency Judicial Order, and it had a big case number, and since we no longer have our copy, I can't look it up.

You know how once you get hooked on Harry Potter and you can't put it down? That was us. We kept saying crap like: did you see this? or listen to this. I can't give you the whole document here, but I'll give you most of the good parts:

*There were four known polluters including KSR, Possum Plating, Seahorse Boats, and the Tom Miller property.

*The judge estimated the percentage of pollution for each and KSR totaled 97 per cent if you included the Miller property and 96 percent if you didn't.

*The plumes of known pollution extended from KSR at the South West corner of the industrial park north through Sunnyside Subdivision.

*A plume of Chromium extended from the former Possum Plating until it merged with the KSR plume on the North East corner of the industrial park.

*The Seahorse and Miller plumes cannot be discriminated from the KSR plume.

*Possum Plating is no longer in business but the former landowner removed all contaminated fixtures, concrete and soils. In addition, he has paid a $400,000.00 fine to the EPA.

*Barrels and soils have been removed from the Miller property by KSR.

*All parties are ordered to commence clean up in an approved manner immediately, to be monitored by the DNR.

*All parties are barred from suing any other potential party until the clean-up is completed.

*Warren Riegle is held negligent and personally liable for the clean-up.

*A clean, freshwater supply must be run immediately to any affected homeowners at KSR's expense.

*KSR will be responsible for any further well contamination including the city's municipal wells, should the plume reach them.

Those TV judges had nothing on this judge. Heck, Judge Hanthorne from Salem had nothing on this judge, and he hung people based on spectral evidence. You could see he was angry at KSR and Reigle in particular and had the power to do something about it. This was Watergate. We were Woodward and Bernstein.

We went and found our guy and asked if we could have a copy of the judgment. He told us in the future, all documents had to stay in the room, and yes, we could have a copy for twenty cents. Sean said he'd be able to handle it if Kevin's stocks were down that day. Kevin paid the quarter and the guy said we could come back if we needed more.

I was hyped all day, not telling anyone, not even Kristen. We agreed to keep it a secret until Sean presented the order to the class, Tuesday. I wanted the big splash, in front of the class, but that was never going to happen again. I'm betting Sean wanted it way worse. Kevin got it. He simply told everyone what he found. Notice the *he*. I'm surprised he didn't hand out autographed copies in the cafeteria. By the time the class started the next day everyone knew everything.

They were excited and they all wanted to get their hands on it, because it was better evidence than we thought we'd ever find, but it was almost as if it were old news by the time they saw it. Sean called Kevin a jackass a little too loudly, and he had to stay after class.

When we went back to the DNR, because I was a part of this group now, and it didn't hurt to see the guy at the DNR. Sean chewed on Kevin the whole time until I told them both to shut -up. My car. My rules. I was sounding like my mom. Sean whined one more time, and Kevin just mocked him and told him he was smarter than him. I told them I was going to crash the car into a tree if they didn't behave, so they did.

We found lots more little evidences, but no more mind blowing impeach the president stuff. The DNR kept requesting plans and demanding the beginning of the clean-up, but seemingly, KSR was doing nothing. Riegle proposed a plan to build a steam powered electrical generating plant and use the heat to clean the water, but later rescinded it because the heat wouldn't clean the water.

I assumed that was the plant Kristen's crazy lady referred to. Kevin found a memo stating the DNR's position would be that the power plant partnering with the city would be a conflict of interest. We knew nothing of a partnership and could find no other information linking the two. There were a lot of memos concerning the hiring of an environmental engineering firm to begin plans to clean up the ground water contamination, but they didn't start until a full year after the judge's orders.

I guess that's pretty much it. It was a lot of fun at first rifling through all those boxes searching for manna and mostly finding the same thing over and over with each progressive document getting a little thicker. By the fourth day I knew I didn't want to be a judge, a DNR case worker, and maybe not even Woodward and Bernstein.

CHAPTER 19
PARANOID?

Things got a little weird here. I came home from school one day and there was a guy with a rental car, and he was taking pictures of my house. I knew it was a rental car because it had a little "e" on the back bumper as in Enterprise. He had a beard and it wasn't a good one. I saw him put the camera on the seat as I pulled by the curb. My dad and Mr. Dombrowski got the driveway. I got the street. Beard acted interested in the house across the street, and then, as if he just saw me, asked if I lived in the neighborhood. I nodded yes and considered calling the police.

I wish I had. He said he was from a real estate company, but he kind of slurred the name and I couldn't catch it. I realized later he didn't want me to. He asked if maybe my house was for sale or if I knew of any in the neighborhood. I shook my head no, not allowing this guy within thirty feet of me. I always trust my instincts around guys and this one was a skunk. He asked if it was a nice neighborhood and I nodded.

"Any problems here?"

"No."

"I'm new to town. Any problems a driven real estate man should know about?"

"No."

I think that's what he wanted. Why else would he ask an eighteen-year-old girl if there are any problems in town? Except for the perv thing I guess. But I don't think I'm the sort who attracts pervs. He wanted me to tell him about the problems I knew about in town, the problems we were investigating.

"Are you just home from school?"

I felt like running. Yes, I nodded still not giving him one word. But just then Mr. Dombrowski turned onto our street. As he parked his car, the man excused himself and casually got into his. It was surreal. Mr. Dombrowski gathered up all his papers and books and was slow getting out. The guy was just as slow leaving, and I didn't move. Everything felt like a bad déjà vu experience.

"What's wrong, Lauren?" Mr. Dombrowski asked. I think I shook my head no, which sounds stupid. He looked from me to the car and back as the guy slowly pulled away. "Who's that?"

"He says he's a real estate guy."

"And he isn't?"

"I don't think so."

"What did he say? Why are you so upset?"

That seemed stupid. I never said I was upset.

"I'm not upset."

"Look at your arms." I looked down and saw them crossed tightly at my chest. Even my feet were crossed. I quickly uncrossed all of them.

"He was taking pictures of my house and asking me if I knew of any problems in town. It didn't seem right."

That was probably the best day I ever had with Mr. Dombrowski. He didn't hug me or put his arm on my shoulder or anything, which would have been all right. But he didn't. We sat on Grandma's steps, and we talked for almost two hours, but it seemed really short. We talked about the man.

"Don't worry," Mr. D, said. "Even if the guy is a private investigator, we have done nothing wrong and this is, after all, America."

We talked about our KSR story and we laughed when we discussed what I would do with my extra credit points. We talked about what I wanted out of life, what made me happy, my fears which I never tell anyone, not even Kristen.

"What books have you read," he asked

The short list didn't impress him.

"There are a few you need to read," he said, "including *Catcher in the Rye*."

I did read it this summer. Holden Caulfield was just like me only he talks a lot more, does stupider things, and doesn't seem to love his parents or anyone except Phoebe. See, inside, he was just like me.

"What makes you happy?" I asked Mr. Dombrowski, because he usually just joked off any personal questions at school.

For a moment, he answered seriously. "I love the school, or at least all the kids. It's an honor that all the parents entrusted them to me, and I'm trying hard to live up to that honor. I like the town and am looking forward to spending a summer here. I like the pizza slices at G&D."

The last part was serious because I knew he ate pizza, too many pizzas judging by the boxes. He had started packing on a few pounds and he knew it. Twice in the fall and once right after Christmas I saw him take off jogging in his little running shorts, blowing cold air. He wasn't gone long either time. I thought of running with him, but what would I do? Just start running alongside? Plus, I hate running, though I know I should run.

And he might think I was watching him. That was a good day.

I'm sure Beard worked for Riegle. I got called down to the office by Silvers, who wanted to know what I wanted with KSR special assessment papers. He was direct and intimidating, and I almost sucked in my breath. The only way he could have known is through the city, because my name was on the FOIA. I took a lesson from Kristen. I smiled at him and kept saying, "special assessment, special assessment" over and over as if I were searching for his answer which I kind of was, since I knew that I had to lie, but I didn't know how big of a lie. I finally said, "Can you be more specific? I have requested so much information from so many places I just can't be sure." I continued to smile.

"Why do you want information on KSR?" he asked.

"They're that really big company in the industrial park, right?"

"Yes."

I just kept smiling. I could tell him what they were doing. Tell him about the Millers or Mrs. Fortuni or Kristen's aunt. But I don't think that's what he wanted to hear. "And this was a special assessment?" I asked again. If I weren't so scared, it might have been fun playing Kristen.

"You requested it at the city offices."

I think he expected me to fold and say, "Oh, that document." Instead I tried to think what would Kristen do, which made me picture those little "What Would Jesus Do?" bracelets that were so popular at one time, and I wondered if "What Would Kristen Do?" bracelets would be as popular. I could hear her: "How could you know about that request?" and maybe he would fold. I overheard one time that if you got called to Silver's office, talk football and he'd forget whatever you were called there for. I didn't know anything about football except Jake. I kept smiling and I'm not a natural smiler.

"You aren't going to answer are you?" he said.

I smiled and restrained from shaking my head no.

"Did Mr. Dombrowski put you up to this? Is it for the newspaper class?"

"Mr. Dombrowski had nothing to do with it." And I said that with conviction. In many ways that was true. He gave us the opportunity and the support, but it was our story. We started it. We found the truth. Our story. I even started to get a little mad that this guy who didn't seem to be half as smart as most of us, and half as concerned as any of us, could spend his time and my time protecting KSR, who was poisoning all of us. What about educating us? Was he out to get Mr. Dombrowski? I got up and left and he never said a word. It felt good being Kristen.

That evening I waited for Mr. Dombrowski on his steps. He was really late and my dad asked me what I was doing and I pointed to the book I was holding. I had to warn him. When he arrived, I told him what happened

"Did you lie?"

"Not really."

"That's good. Lying would make it worse when we do print the stories. I got called in today too. I told Silvers I had heard you filed an FOIA for something but never got anything back, so apparently it was never going to amount to anything."

"That's mostly true," I said.

"That's what I went with," he said.

"Maybe we shouldn't print anything about KSR. After all, the people in Sunnyside are getting clean water and the judge had ordered a clean-up."

"It's always easy to rationalize an easy solution but

difficult to do what is right." He reminded me of Mrs. Fortuni, the other ill people, Mrs. Miller who was probably going to lose her house, and if it weren't for the people in the DNR who did the right thing, wouldn't KSR still be spreading their pollution?

"I knew nothing about newspapers," he said, "when I started the class, but I learned that Jefferson and Madison intended the free press to be the fourth estate of government, the one who oversees the other three and makes sure they fulfill their roles in protecting the welfare of the citizens. If we don't shine a light on KSR, what is to stop the next KSR?"

He didn't seem scared at all.

I warned Kristen that she might be called down to the office, but she never was. Silvers knew better.

CHAPTER 20
D.S.

The city questioned everyone. Somebody (it had to be Riegle) wanted to know who told the kids from school what documents to request. Colbert's source said all personnel who had handled the special assessment were called into the city manager's office and grilled about what they thought about the special assessment. When asked, she answered that it seemed like an ideal solution. She's no idiot. I thought the whole thing sounded a lot like Silvers calling me to the office. Was he expecting one of them to break and say, "I hate it so much that I gave it to kids so they could print it in their high school newspaper. Please don't give me detention."

She told Colbert, "Follow up on the owners of the power plant, but go through the DNR, not the city. I promise you, you'll be surprised." She really didn't seem happy.

I had the documents. From the city. They had arrived that day along with a bill for $1.55. I wondered if they could even recoup their billing cost by actually charging for them. I called Kristen and highlighted some of the stuff I had read. She told me to bring them over, but I had to pick up Colbert first. They really were his documents. I didn't want to pick him up, and I sure didn't want to call him. So Kristen called him, which I'm sure was a thrill, and then she called me and said he'd be ready by the time I got there. I couldn't guess what it would take for Colbert to get ready.

He lives in not exactly the best part of town. I don't mean it's dangerous, but a lot of the houses are lacking paint. He came out just as I pulled up, which was a relief for both of us. I don't need a lot of details here but he stunk, not as in unclean, but as in cologne. I didn't know if Kristen had told him that he and I were going on a date, a three way, or the truth, but he was way over prepared. I cracked the window—about six inches.

So, I went from my house, to Colbert's, to Kristen's. Kristen was poor. It was a tiny house in a series of small houses and mobile homes with roofs built over the top. Kristen's mother says some day she's going to get lucky and find some change on the way to work and they can move up to lower, lower, lower middle class. When I parked, I made Colbert sit for over a minute while I checked the mirrors to see if we were followed. I admit I was a little paranoid.

Kristen lived there with her mother and little sister whose name is Charly. Colbert said, "Carly?" and Kristen said, "No, just Charly," and she said it in a way that meant "don't even go there."

Who the heck names their daughter Charly? I could see she was already a miniature version of Kristen only quieter. She sat by us the whole evening taking in everything we said, hardly ever saying a word. I think she understood some of the stuff a lot faster than Kristen, but that might be because she nodded her head a lot. So, I never talked, Charly almost never talked, Kristen never stopped talking, and Colbert was beaming as if Kristen's house was a little bit of heaven. The whole thing was surreal.

I got out the documents, handed one to Colbert and Kristen told him to shut up and read it. We could see almost no difference in any of the three versions, but there was a lot of good stuff in them. Plus, the last one obviously had a Post-it note stuck to it, which got copied right in with the document.

So I read the first one first again. It began with a bunch of legal jargon stating that a governmental body such as the city has the authority to render a special assessment to benefit the community. Then it noted that this was a resolution that would provide such benefit by taxing all properties in the Harry Canton Industrial Park brownfield. The special tax would be used to clean any and all pollutants from the soil and groundwater in the industrial park. I hadn't even known that it was called the Harry Canton Industrial Park. Canton was a congressman from our town who was supposed to have been a real Horatio Algiers story back in the 20' and 30's. He went to Washington a poor man and came back rich. Big deal. Who doesn't? The assessment was intended to run a filtration plant that was to be funded through revenue bonds and paid for by the collection of a special tax on the KSR Energy plant, which would be exempt from paying property taxes.

I stopped there. "Do you guys know what that means?"

Kristen said no.

"I think, so far," said Colbert, "they are going to charge everyone for cleaning up what was mostly KSR's mess, and the new power plant is going to pay for the clean-up facility."

"What's is wrong with the second part," Kristen asked.

"Those taxes normally would have gone to the entire

community, to benefit the community. Now they are basically just benefiting KSR. Our town will get the smoke, downstate gets the electricity, and KSR basically gets the money. My secret source said we need to follow up on who owns the plant."

I gave him a funny look, like he shouldn't emphasize "secret source" out loud, but Charly perked right up.

Kristen pointed ahead to the money in the document. "The projected expense of running the facility is almost $200,000 per year and the special assessment could last as long as forty years, renewable every five years. Property owners are divided into two categories: tier 1 and tier 2. Tier 2 properties are labeled Potentially Responsible Parties (PRP's) by the DNR and will be taxed at ten times the rate as the tier 1 properties. The tier 2 properties were KSR, Tom Miller property, Possum Plating and Seahorse Boats. There is a provision for adding Tier 2's should it become necessary. Yeah. Yeah. Yeah," and pointed further down the page. "Both Possum Plating and Seahorse Boats are paying more than KSR, more than twice as much. They charged by how much property someone owns."

"By the acreage?"

"Yes."

"But that means the Millers have to pay half as much as a huge corporation," Colbert said. "Twenty thousand will bankrupt the Millers but twice that is nothing to KSR. It's like you could have a little piece of crap house....," and Colbert stopped right there, obviously trying not to look around. When Kristen didn't seem to notice, he continued, "So tax on a dump little house on a full acre will be twice as much as a mansion on a half acre."

"Boy Colbert. That's why we brought you here tonight. We knew you were smart but nothing like that."

I guess Kristen had noticed.

"Well who wrote this thing? It's almost like KSR wrote it themselves, or someone at the city wrote it to make it as cheap as possible for them."

"That's what I think. Lauren, don't you think so?"

I nodded yes.

"You can't be serious."

"Right around the middle of the third page, right there," Kristen said pointing to a paragraph she wanted him to read. I think he gave four "holy craps" as he read it. Basically it said the city agreed to reimburse KSR for all expenses incurred for their environmental engineering firm, their running water mains to Sunnyside subdivision, and barrel and soil clean up on the Miller property. That was the first three craps then the big one. The reimbursement was over a million dollars.

"Impressive huh? Now read the bottom of the last paragraph, last page, the part that is crossed out."

I read where it said that the city shall be liable for cleaning up any later discovered pollution plumes created by a Tier 2 company within the city limits.

"But that is blatant," Colbert said. "If we know KSR has barrels buried all over the city, the city must know it too. That has to be why someone crossed it out."

"Two things, Brain Boy. First, why would the city ever write that in a proposal?"

"I thought of that. They simply wouldn't."

"Right. And if you look at the last paragraph of the second document, that proposal is gone. But if you look at the third, and near as we can tell, final document, it's back."

And there it was.

"How could they ever propose this? They'll never get it through the city commission."

"It looks like they are going to try. See where the

Post-it note was stuck on the final copy?"

It said: APPROVED. NOTIFY W.R., D.S. AND LEGAL It was signed J. Walker.

"J. Walker is the city manager. I met him," I said. "He's an ego in a suit."

"I am willing to bet that W.R. is Warren Riegle," Colbert said.

"Lauren and I guessed that too, but we don't have a clue who D.S. is."

"I don't know anything of a D.S. I might be able to check with my source but she is getting a little nervous. Are there any other changes between the three documents?"

"We didn't read them page for page but if you hold them next to each other we only found spelling changes and the numbers vary a little. The final document lists all the tier 1's and how much they are going to have to pay. Some of them are almost $4,000 a year and they didn't even pollute."

Colbert skimmed the third document and noticed the bottom of the last page had a cc. list, which is an old term for carbon copy. Listed were W.R., J.W., and Campbell, et. al. "D.S. wrote the special assessment."

"How do you know?"

Colbert pointed to the Campbell on the last page. "Campbell, Campbell and LeBaron are the city's law firm and if they get a copy, they didn't write it. Same with Riegle and Walker. And Walker had to notify D. S. that he approved this copy."

Kristen quickly covered Charly's ears. "Damn Colbert. You are smart. But how are we going to prove who D. S. is?"

"The internet," Charly said.

"You didn't hear that. I had my hands over your ears. And what are we going to do? Type in D. S. and out will come our author."

"You swore."

"Okay, so you heard me." She gave her a nudge and you could tell they were close.

Let's all swear together," Colbert said and we all gave him a weird look. I think he wanted a nudge too. "Or not then. "Do you have internet here?" He sounded doubtful.

"My mom wouldn't be without it. She does internet personal ads and meets all these internet losers. But you still can't type in D. S. and get his name."

"He has to work for KSR and KSR is a large corporation so they have to have a website. If this guy is a big wig working for them he's probably listed."

Kristen popped up, "Let's check."

Charly was right behind her and I was one step back. Colbert followed us and realized we were going into a bedroom. Maybe Kristen's bedroom? A holy site. He froze at the door. What kind of bragging rights did that entail? I think he began to sweat.

"Don't touch anything or sit on the bed. Mom's really anal."

I think that eliminated any bragging rights since you can't tell anyone you were in the bedroom of the mother of the prettiest girl in school.

That computer must have taken ten minutes to turn on and connect to the internet. Dial up. I didn't know it still existed. I thought it was just a little creepy sitting on the floor listening to any sound waiting for Kristen's mother to come charging in wanting to know what the hell a boy was doing in her bedroom. Or worse. Wanting to thank Kristen for bringing a boy to her bedroom. I looked for places to hide.

Kristen finally got the thing open to KSR's webpage and there he was, David Stevens, chief legal-council, executive vice president, and board member. Gotcha! Group hug. Colbert way too enthusiastic.

"But we still can't use Stevens' name unless we get another source," Kristen said, ruining our party.

"We'll figure out a way," Colbert said finally relinquishing the last of his grip on our waists.

When we were done, I gave him a ride home, and he kept trying to talk to me. Not that he wasn't nice. I just didn't feel like talking.

But true to her word, Kristen gave Colbert full credit. We presented our new evidence as a group. No Cadillacs, grandmas, gold stars, or nakedness. Just Kristen, Colbert and me up front with the best evidence our class had found yet.

CHAPTER 21
MARCH EDITION OR WHAT'S A ZMUDZINSKI

Understand that by this time we had a lot of solid evidence on KSR and had printed nothing. We could show they polluted all over town until they were forced to stop, ordered by a federal judge to clean it up, basically ignored the judge's order while they concocted a plan to have others pay the majority of the costs, while according to the judge they did 97% of the damage. They would profit from a power plant that would not pay normal taxes, and the city would be reimbursing them over a million dollars. How could all this go on in a small town and no one know about it?

Instead, we printed our March edition. I think it was our worst. Other than that big article on the Carnegie Library that included about ten oversize pictures so that it filled up all of the front page and part of the second, it had nothing. Even Sean laid off on the book reviews by writing on Steinbeck's *East of Eden*. Nobody could criticize that because nobody else is going to read that thing having been force fed *Grapes of Wrath*. The fambly must stick together. The fambly must stick together. Die Okies! Die! Why do schools do this to kids?

Kristen wrote her advice column on selecting the right college, and Jake interviewed the new assistant track coach who worked with the throwers. I guess for like one week in college one time he had thrown his shot-put further than anyone else. Then someone threw it further and he tore a ligament in his knee. Who cares? I'll tell you. Silvers cared. The day after the paper came out, Silvers was in the room telling us what a great paper it was. Keep up the good work. Maybe you could do an article on the baseball coach because he once had a tryout with the Toronto Bluejays. Etcetera. Etcetera. Etcetera. Who cares about the Toronto Bluejays, or even baseball? Here was Silvers complimenting us on what we all knew was our worst paper, and the only other time he had been in our room was to confiscate our Abou edition, my personal favorite.

Silvers almost caught us doing real work. Kevin and Sean were reading the permit application for Eagle Power, the electric power plant we thought was owned by KSR. They had just obtained it from the DNR by going there without me. Both froze when the door opened and Silvers walked in and they just edged back to seats as he talked. Good job. Carry on. Keep up the good work. Etcetera. Etcetera. Etcetera. He must have gone to some false praise, feel good seminar. He never complimented any of our good work. Why start now? There was lots of anger once he left until Mr. D. brought us back. He said Mr. Silvers was doing his job so let's do ours.

Sean was putting on a show. He was determined not to be upstaged by Kevin again. Being coal fired, the plant was going to put out a lot of smoke and particulates, but the permit was based on the latest technologies including strippers.

"My source, notice the his and not his and Kevin's, said it was all upfront, modern, and approved. The problem with coal fired plants is the mercury and the acid rain, even with the strippers. The prevailing winds will gradually make the fish in Round Lake virtually unsafe, but he personally wouldn't eat fish from most of the lakes east of California." Sean paused to make sure we all got that. But he said it was a good plant and such is the cost of electricity. No real story there.

"Now, drum roll please," and he looked at Kevin who did nothing. Dramatic silence then, "KSR doesn't own the plant. It is funded by an Eastern conglomerate, and it lists Warren Riegle as the principle owner. No surprise there. And three silent partners."

Another dramatic pause.

"Come on, Sean," Kevin begged, but not too hard, since he knew he shut out Sean last time.

"All right, but you guys are going to love this. Twenty percent goes to Colbert's David Stevens. Way to go Colbert." Colbert stood up and bowed. His bow-tie, a clip-on, came loose on one side and hung down. "And twenty percent goes to-o-o-o-o-o the city. Yes, our dear city donated the land for the plant and in return, partnered with the devil."

There was an audible collective sigh, clearly begun by the brighter kids, and rapidly caught on by the others. It was checkmate. In order to avoid the judge's order and minimize their expense, they made the city a full partner. It guaranteed their special assessment and privileged tax abatement on the plant.

Sean said, "That's some catch, that Catch-22." Nobody got it. Nobody laughed, so he said, "It's a line from *Catch-22* after the establishment perfectly screwed everyone else. They did it here. If you have no decency, you can almost admire the genius of Riegle."

"That's why no one will help the Millers," Erin said. "Or anyone else."

Kristen followed with, "Mr. Dombrowski, we have to print it now. It can't wait if we are going to help anyone."

There were several yeses that followed, and everyone looked at him. He sat there on the edge of his desk
and looked at his hands, not at Kristen or anyone else.
It was almost with a tone of resignation after a long
pause that he simply said, "It's time."

Anna had already been on the calendar for the April
edition and she began outlining the pages. Everyone
was excited because this is what American journalism
is supposed to be about. Stories and page editors were
assigned. A chart was put on the board with a promise
to Mr. D. that it would be erased before the hour was
out. People lined up at the three working computers and
asked Matt when the fourth would be ready. Mr. D. cau-
tioned us that every single fact needed absolute docu-
mentation. No errors of fact were allowed. And not
even a single typo. That would be a record.

Everyone was scattering around and lost in it all
were Sean and Kevin. Sean was trying to get everyone's
attention, but it was Kevin's whistle that stopped us.
"Sean," he said graciously giving the floor back to
Sean. They must have worked something out because
Kevin was a jerk 364 days a year. "There was a third
silent partner. It is something called Eagle Enterprises
Limited. The guy at the DNR said we could go to the
courthouse and find who registered that name. Kevin
and I went there yesterday after school and found that
it is a new company, less than a year old, and it is owned
by a John and Martha Zmudzinski of Phoenix, Arizona.
We Googled in both their names and Eagle Enterprises
and got nothing but a home phone number for the
Zmudzinskis. Nothing from Eagle. We don't have a
clue where to go from here, but maybe it's not important."

"With a name like that living in Arizona, they could

be on the government's witness protection program,"
Kristen said. "Anyone else would have changed it."

BryananderiN became obsessed with finding out
who the Zmudzinski's were. They figured since everything else about the deal was dirty, they had to be too.
But they could find nothing. I went back to the courthouse with them just in hopes of finding something
Sean and Kevin missed, but all we got was their name,
number and address, same as Sean.

Erin wanted to call them and say, "Are you John and
Martha Zmudzinski who own Eagle Enterprises?" but
then what do you say? You can't ask them how they
own a company way up here. You can't even ask if they
own any other power plants, because it won't tell us
what we need to know. We tried looking up marriage
licenses. No Zmudzinski's. We went to the public library and rifled the genealogy files. I say rifled because
they looked like someone had shot them up long before
we got there. Nothing.

One day, almost a week after Sean read the permit,
Bryan was at Erin's killing time after school. His coach
had canceled cc practice because he had a dentist ap-
pointment and told them to individually do a three-mile
speed regiment. That's where you jog a block, sprint a
block, jog a block, sprint a block. Basically, he sprinted
right over to Erin's. Her mom left them to run errands
and told them they needed to be there when the devil's
spawn came home on the bus. Of course, she called her
Erica. Only Erin called her devil's spawn and only
when her parents weren't around. I don't think her
mother ever worried about Bryan and she was probably
right.

Bryan was playing on the computer when Erica got
home with a friend who Erin said was a neighbor's kid
who stayed there until one of her parents came home

from work. So Erin was limiting their cookie intake, and Bryan was failing miserably at finding a Zmudzinski link, when he called to Erin that maybe Zmudzinski was a pseudonym and not a real name.

The little kid with Erica said, "That's my grandma and grandpa's name." When Bryan told the story he used the little kid's voice.

"I said Zmudzinski, with a Z."

"That's why most of his friends call him Grandpa, Z. And Grandma is Mrs. Z. But it's really Zmudzinski."

"Are you a Zmudzinski?" Erin asked.

"No," she laughed as if that was a stupid question.

"Kelli," at least Erin knew her first name. "Do your grandparents live in Arizona?"

"Yes, but my Grandpa Walker lives in Wisconsin. Grandma Walker is in Heaven."

It probably took Bryan about twelve seconds to figure out why the name Walker was familiar, but Erin had it in a nanosecond. "Is your name Walker and does your dad work for the city?"

"Of course it's Walker. Kelli Z Walker only the Z doesn't stand for anything. Just Z. And my dad is the boss of the city."

Bryan signaled Erin into the other room and she left the cookie bag unattended. He watched over her shoulder as the devil's spawn filled a pocket, all the time vigilantly checking the back of Erin's head so she wouldn't get caught. "We got him," he said when they couldn't hear us.

"No we don't. It's unlikely, but there could be lots of Zmudzinski's in Arizona."

"It's too big of a coincidence."

"But we can't print anything on a coincidence."

"How are we going to prove that her grandparents, parents-in-law of the city manager, are the ones who own twenty percent of Eagle Power?"

"She could call," Erin said as she poked him hard in the ribs. She did that a lot.

"Okay. So we call this number for the Zmudzinski's who own Eagle Enterprises Limited, hand her the phone and she says what?"

"'Hi,' Silly. It's her grandparents."

So that's what we did. We dialed the number we got from the courthouse, handed the phone to Kelli, and she said, "Hi, Grandma. It's me Kelli." And they proceeded to have a great conversation.

CHAPTER 22
MOM

Erin said we were lucky, like God wanted us to learn that Eagle Enterprises, the Zmudzinski's, and James Walker, City Manager were basically one in the same. I don't know if God had anything to do with it, or even luck. We did good work, and I don't think Walker ever expected anyone to even try to trace ownership of the plant, so he didn't hide it all that well. Erin always gives God a lot of credit which I guess is okay. Although we really couldn't prove that Mr. Walker personally was the partial owner of the power plant, any reader could figure it out.

The class decided we couldn't print how we made the Walker/Zmudzinski connection, because we did kind of take advantage of a little kid. Randy was given the story to write, which was only fair since he got kind of shut out because he hated KSR early. Now everyone hated them. Probably the only thing we hated more was the city. They're supposed to be held to a high standard, and near as we could tell, they made it all possible for Riegle and KSR to profit millions from the power plant and avoid paying millions in clean-up costs. It's always about money. Creeps.

I got home from school and had a message from Doris Miller to call her. My mom wanted to know who she was, and I told her I was interviewing her for a story but didn't go into details. Never give parents any details is my motto.

Mrs. Miller, my mom was right there, so I had to call her Mrs. Miller, wanted to know if we had printed our paper yet. Why was she calling me and not Erin? When I told her not yet, she said she needed help.

"If only Tom (her husband) were here. Warren would never do this to Tom," she said.

"What are they trying to do now, Mrs. Miller?"

"Call me Doris. I just got this letter in the mail today saying that they are holding the special assessment public hearing next Tuesday night at the city hall. If I oppose the assessment, I either have to be there or have an attorney put it in writing. I can't afford an attorney."

"What do you want me to do?" I almost said Doris but my mom hadn't turned a page in her book so she was probably listening in. I needed to get off the phone.

"If you hurry up and print your paper and let everyone know what they are doing to Tommy and me, I think lots of people will come to the meeting. Then they'd have to listen and vote it down."

"Doris," I said her name in almost a whisper and my mom stirred a little. "We are working as hard as we can on that paper. There are a lot of articles we are writing and editing. We still need the pictures of everything and they need to be Photoshopped. We've got an ad team out raising the money to print the paper, but I don't think it will be out before late April. I'm sorry."

"Why are they doing this to us, Lauren?" Now she was crying. I've got to tell you, I'm not even good when it's kids who are crying. I couldn't reach the chips on the table. I needed chips. Why are we the last family in America to get portable phones? So I did nothing.

"They're not just doing this to you. While others

may not be losing their house, everybody in the city loses if this passes." I felt in my pockets for anything.

"Tommy says he will burn down the house the day we are forced out. They'd probably send him to jail, and even though the house looks a little dated, I'll admit, I still love it and don't want to see anything happen to it. It's a shame Tom's not alive. I've thought about just staying in it and letting them come in and drag an old woman out. Besides, where would I go?"

"I will go to the meeting," I said and couldn't believe that was me talking. "I'll get as many kids as I can from the newspaper class and we'll all speak against the special assessment. It has to help."

"God bless you child." Now God was getting credit for me going to a meeting, which had to be one of the last things I wanted to do.

After hanging up, my mom wanted to know what was going on. I tried to avoid the details part again but she wanted to know how everyone in the city loses if something passes. I reminded her she taught me that it wasn't nice listening in on other people's conversations. She told me to quit trying to change the subject and tell her what was going on.

I didn't know what to say. This was my mom, and she would throw a fit if she even guessed I was doing anything wrong. And this would certainly be wrong in her eyes. Plus, we all agreed not to tell our parents. I told her I needed some quick food and then to do homework, a really big test tomorrow. I lied. I saw Oreos in the pantry, but they were almost half gone and the pantry was the other side of mom. I thought I would just leave but my mom stopped me.

"Lauren, are you in some kind of trouble?"

"No."

"Who is this woman you called Doris?" and she

emphasized Doris as in reminding me I am not to call adults by their first name.

"She's just a lady we're doing a story about."

"Is she in trouble?"

"Yes. Kind of. But she hasn't done anything wrong."

"Why did she call you?"

"I'm helping Erin with the story."

"What's the story about?"

"I really can't say."

"Can't or won't? And you should be eating fruit. Have an apple."

"No Thanks." I had been eating chips without realizing it and now they tasted blah.

"Can't or won't? You didn't answer."

"We all agreed not to tell our parents or anyone."

"Has anyone told?"

"I don't know. I don't think so."

"So maybe some of them have told but the parents kept the secret?"

"Maybe."

"I wouldn't even tell your father so long as I think you've done nothing wrong. It's not dangerous, is it?"

"No," I said with much more reassurance than I felt.

"Then tell me."

I thought I could tell her just a little to leave me alone, but I couldn't stop. I told her pretty much everything except the Erica/Zmudzinski thing because we still felt a little guilty about that.

She kept nodding her head and questioning, "Are you sure this is accurate? And this is going on in our town? This can't be true; why hasn't any of this been in the paper? You did all this for school?" until I finished with the partners in the plant. I didn't tell her about thinking I was being followed or getting called down to Silver's office.

"You're sure everything you said is accurate?"

"We have two sources or official documents to prove everything."

"And you've been right in the middle of this?"

"Pretty much the whole thing," I said again avoiding the Erica thing.

"You know Lauren. When you edited that one paper that the principal destroyed, I didn't talk to you and I should have. I thought about marching down to that asshole's office and giving him two or three pieces of my mind hurting my little girl like that. But you wouldn't have liked that?"

"No," I said slowly shaking my head visualizing it.

"I should have at least told you I was proud of you. That was a beautiful paper and there was nothing wrong with that stupid little tattoo on the front page," she sighed. "This time I'm going to tell you, Lauren," she held my chin and looked straight in my eyes. "I have never been prouder of you. You are turning into a terrific young lady." I was glad she didn't cry here. My throat felt like I swallowed an elephant and my eyes were at emergency flood stage. At least she didn't try any of that motherly hug stuff like if it were a sitcom. We're really not a hugging family.

"You've got to try to help Mrs. Miller."

I nodded first because I didn't want to lose it. "I'm going to go to the meeting." Pause. "I'm guessing if we get a bunch of us there it can help."

"It's something."

"And we are going to print everything in the next paper. I'm just afraid it will be too late for Mrs. Miller."

"Can I help at all?" This woman looked a lot like my mom.

"Just by keeping it a secret, even from Daddy. And maybe you could put some gas in my car."

I can't say that mom and I were ready to live happily ever after, or that it was the start of a better relationship, but it was good knowing that mom thought we were doing the right thing and she was on our side.

CHAPTER 23
MAYOR OF FROWNSVILLE

Kristen had to threaten to quit her job at Subway in order to get Tuesday night off to attend the special assessment meeting. And Tuesdays are Two for Tuesdays, which isn't quite like it sounds, because you do pay extra for the second sandwich, but One-and-a-half for Tuesday has no magic to it and probably wouldn't draw the crowds. Her boss didn't want to give her the night off because he would have to take her place on the line, but she reminded him she never took nights off and sells a lot of subs in that place just being there. He knew she was right.

Most of us who were heavily involved were there. BryananderiN and Randy and Sean and Anna and Colbert and even Matt. I admit, I was a psycho by then thinking I saw Beard, the fake real estate guy almost everywhere.

Kristen reveled in the whole thing. She made fun of the mayor who started the meeting with the pledge of allegiance. Apparently, he was "the bald gnome guy with the bird's nest toupee."

He opened the meeting with roll call. There were only seven of them and they had their names in front of their chairs. If there had been an empty chair he could have just written down the name and said, "Obviously

Joe Blow is missing tonight," and then maybe made a joke about how he didn't see Mrs. Joe Blow there either. But he took about ten minutes calling off those names one at a time and listening for a reply making a comment with each. Finally, he called off Mayor Roger Khronberg and said, "I'm present," as if that were his private laugh with the little people in the audience. Some laughed.

He turned to our small group. "I can see we have a number of students with us tonight. You are always welcome. After the meeting, if you would like your agendas signed for Government credit, please see Linda who is recording everything we say." He pointed to a lady who sat on the side of the commissioners, and he gave us a sweeping smile. He had no clue why we were there.

Then they still didn't start. They had to approve the minutes from the last meeting. When Mayor Gnome asked for approval it was like he woke everyone up. They all scrambled through their folders looking like they were double-checking their corrections when it was obvious none of them had read them ahead of time. Ten more minutes.

Then we did an abatement for a company who wanted to buy a new big piece of equipment that they promised would add about a million jobs in our town. Okay, not a million, but it was like the entire thing was choreographed with scripts and hidden strings funneling all the way over to James Walker, the ego in a suit, who stood on the sidelines nodding his approval as each commissioner voted their yay with no comment or dissension. Who says yay or nay? Of course, it was Kristen sitting next to me waiting to jump up and say something who pointed out the strings.

"Can't you see them Lauren. Little pulleys and

strings. Right to his fingers." I almost could.

There were four of these things that came up for a vote and they all passed the same way, unanimously. We really were an hour into it and Mayor Gnome was still smiling at everyone. I can smile, but I can't match his endurance. Randy was getting restless and looked like he was going to blow. He looked calm compared to Tommy. Erin said she was going to sit by Mrs. Miller, and she and Bryan were holding hands next to her and a fully grown adult boy. It had to be Tommy. He wore a suit he didn't look totally comfortable in. I was too nervous to eat my Three Musketeers.

There probably weren't twenty-five people in the whole audience, and I noticed each time a special favor was granted by the king, one or two of them left, satisfied with their largesse. Mrs. Neihardt would be proud of largesse. I discovered that the mayor could smile while drinking water, Colbert had new glasses and cleaned them a lot. And why do only old or desperate people run for city commission? You have to be half dead to live through the meetings.

Finally, our time came.

Mayor Gnome spoke up and said he would open public comment on the proposed Special Assessment 24. We all fidgeted. In unison, the commissioners all turned their folders and pulled out a stapled document that looked a lot like the one we had, from where I sat. I checked to see if J. Walker could avoid moving his fingers or lips like a master puppeteer.

The Ego who had so much to gain spoke up first. He addressed the commission. "Let me explain the purpose behind this Special Assessment. We have some problems involving water contamination in the industrial park, which limit the future growth of our community's industries, and unless we take a bold and innovative solution, we will face years of litigation and possibly decades of stagnation. Businesses may relocate, and there is a possibility that we could lose our well field, which supplies all of the water to the city unless we act quickly."

"So you are supporting this Special Assessment?" the mayor without a brain asked.

Even the Ego was taken back by that question but he held on and said, "Yes Mr. Mayor, I am."

"And you say that if we don't pass this it will lead to years of litigation."

"Yes. No one can say for sure just how much pollution is down there and who is responsible for what or how much, so this was the simplest and fairest compromise we could come up with. Without this, one company may sue another, then another, etc., until decades have passed with no clean up."

"And what would happen if the pollution hit our city well fields?" This was so choreographed, plus we knew under the judge's orders, KSR was responsible for those wells and had done 97 percent of the pollution.

"If that were to happen, Mr. Mayor, it may well bankrupt our city. We have eight wells there with a replacement cost of one half million dollars each plus the infrastructure and land. We must act quickly on this assessment." I am telling you, he never flinched. I've told a few lies, but never with his level of sincerity. He had to practice.

"Anything else, Mr. Walker?"

"No, I will be here to answer any questions that may arise."

"Okay. We will open our forum now. Everyone will be given an opportunity to speak. No vote will be held tonight but it will be scheduled for our next regular board meeting, the first Tuesday in May."

A big man in a dark suit stood up. "Will you state your name and your business please sir?" Mr. Bird's Nest Mayor said.

"I am Phil Hutzel, attorney representing Sims Industrial."

"Yes sir?"

"We are listed as a tier one property and being taxed $3,847 per year. We accept that but we have a concern."

"Yes sir?" still grinning.

"While we have always believed in being a good neighbor to our community and have an outstanding environmental record, it being utmost in our concern, there have been over the years any number of minor spills of various chemicals, all of which we cleaned as rapidly as we were made aware of them. While we do not object to our current standing as a tier one, we do object to later being classified as a tier two, as our payment would be higher than some of the major tier twos due to our acreage."

"Um, Mr. Walker, would you like to handle this?"

"Yes sir, I can. Mr. Hutzel, we are not and will not be looking for any more tier two properties. With passage of this assessment, we will be in good financial shape and ready to move into the future. I would not mention any spills again no matter how minor." I couldn't help but think he was talking of his financial shape and a future move maybe to Bermuda.

"Then Sims Industrial has no objection to the special assessment."

"Thank you sir. Will there be any further comments or is that it?" said the toupeed comb-over mayor.

I looked at Erin as she nudged Doris but it was Tommy who jumped up. "I object!" he said. Too much TV.

"There's nothing to object to, sir. Can you state your

name and business to the commission?" Still smiling.

"My name's Tom Miller." He said it with a certain pride as if everyone should know he was and maybe be a little afraid. "In many ways my business is dirt."

"Dirt?"

"Yes. During the summers I work mostly in landscaping and what I'm saying is I was there every day when those barrels were removed from my mama's yard and that dirt was clean. I held it in my hand and smelled it. Hell, you could eat that dirt."

"Son, I have to warn you to watch your language or you will be removed."

"Yes sir, I will."

"Are you talking about the Tom Miller property now owned by Doris Miller?" the chief puppeteer asked.

"She's my momma."

"I'm right here."

"It's okay Momma. I'll handle this."

"That property is listed as a PRP by the DNR. Are you aware of that?" again the puppeteer asked as the commissioners turned from manager to Tommy and back like a tennis match.

"That is what they say, but I was right there and I say the soil was clean and the barrels never leaked."

"You may take that up with the DNR. Our hands are tied." The mayor didn't even try to intervene.

"Your hands aren't tied!" Tommy practically shouted. "You wrote the rules and you can change the rules!"

"Sir, this is the last time I will remind you this is a civil discussion. If we have to, we will remove you." Mayor Smiling Gnome nodded towards the city police officer who didn't appear at all interested in dragging Tommy out of there, as Tommy was easily bigger and built.

"Let me handle it Tommy," his ma said. "I am Doris Miller and I want you to tell everyone present what you are going to do to an old lady who can't pay this assessment."

"Mr. Walker," Mr. That's Too Tough For Me Mayor said looking at him.

"That becomes a matter for the state. If you fall two years behind on your taxes, you forfeit your property and the state will put it up for bids to the highest bidder."

"And what will happen to me?"

"Mrs. Miller. If the city commission passes this assessment next month, you must pay it or you will lose your house."

"I cannot pay it. Your tax is more money than I make. I cannot sell my house, though the good Lord knows that I don't want to, because who would buy a fifty-thousand-dollar house with an extra twenty thousand dollars in taxes each year?"

"So are you objecting to the special assessment?"

"Of course I am as it is written. I know my husband Tom should not have left those barrels there, but I also trust my son Tommy who says they did not spill or leak. I could probably see fit to pay an assessment of maybe $500 a year but I don't even know where that will come from."

"Mrs. Miller, we have worked on this assessment for over six months to make it as fair as possible. You are a tier 2 and will remain as such. We cannot be expected to start over in order to favor one property owner when expediency is an issue. Also, someone else would have to pay your share, and that would not be fair to them."

"Warren Riegle and KSR should pay for my special assessment. Warren always promised he would take care of us, and it was KSR's chemicals. Tom was only doing his job."

"Did you get that in writing from him, Mrs. Miller?"

"No, but he said it many times."

"Do you have any other objections at this time?"

"No."

The Mayor of K-Mart toupee jumped in. He momentarily looked serious but then smiled when he finished. "Your objections are duly noted, but we must move on. Our time for public comment is almost up. Do we have anyone else?"

Erin jumped right up almost shouting before he could close public comment, "I would like to speak." Bryan looked lovesick.

"Yes sweetheart," he said with this paternalistic grin. "You must give your name and business for the record using that wonderful accent of yours. "Is it central Georgia?"

"My name is Erin Morton and I grew up in North Carolina, not Georgia." The Mayor was beginning to look a little lovesick too, and I wondered if he was a pervert, peeking at porn on the internet whenever he thought his wife of eighty years wasn't looking. "What business do you have?"

"I am a member of the public and I am concerned with what you are doing not only to Mrs. Miller here, but the public as a whole."

He covered his microphone but everyone could hear him as he asked the city manager if a member of the public with no real business could talk in a public comment period. He was told to give her two or three minutes at most, as there were still three more items on the agenda.

"We would like you to limit your comments to two or three minutes, Miss Morton. We have a lot of important city business still to discuss."

"I would like to state my objection to the entire special assessment."

"Can she do that James?"

And James the Manager stepped in again to save the Mayor With No Balls. Kristen again. "We will note your objection. Now we must move on."

"I am not finished."

"You only have maybe thirty seconds left."

"This entire special assessment was set up only for the benefit of KSR and Warren Riegle. In fact, is it not true that David Stevens, Vice President and legal counsel for KSR, wrote the special assessment?"

Mr. Mayor without a brain covered his microphone and whispered, "How could she know that?" but most of us could hear. There was some murmuring among the commissioners. There was almost hope they had come to life like Pinocchio.

The Ego in a suit spoke slowly. "Yes, it's true that Mr. Stevens had some input, but so did everyone involved."

"I never got any input," Mrs. Miller said quite loudly.

"I'm sorry, but your comment time is up, just as it is for this young lady. You may sit down." Erin looked hot and frustrated. She nudged Bryan but Colbert stood up first.

"My name is Daryl Scarbrough and I would like to make a comment again as a concerned citizen."

"Our time is limited, young man," Mayor Having Trouble Smiling said.

"You have KSR basically writing a special assessment that minimizes their expense to less than 8% of the total cost of clean-up, while a federal judge has already found them responsible for 97% of the pollution and ordered them to clean it up. You used a special assessment so that Warren Riegle would not have to pay anything." I have to admit Colbert can be an eloquent speaker. His voice was almost booming, filling the meeting room. "You partnered with him on the Eagle Power plant, which leaves you in a conflict of interest. And you, Mr. Walker, through your parents-in-law, are a silent partner in that same firm, and here you are pushing through a tax which benefits your partners, who in turn benefit you."

"Mr. Scarbrough," James the Guilty interrupted. "Personally, I think you've been watching too many Bourne movies or something. You cannot come into a public forum and make unsubstantiated charges. That is libelous and subject to lawsuits. Now we must move on."

"I am not finished. You also…"

"Son," the Mayor with the Nest Which was No Longer on Straight said. "Your time is up, and if you cannot follow protocol you will be removed by our deputy."

"I would like my two minutes," Kristen jumped up and said. "My name is Kristen Rossell, and I too am a concerned citizen." She never gave either of them a chance to paternalize her. "Mr. Walker, you lied to this commission tonight. I don't know if they actually have the right to think for themselves here, but they get to vote next month so they deserve the truth. First, according to the judge's order, these companies may not sue each other. Second,…" The mayor tried to gavel her down here. "Second, if the city wells go bad, KSR is responsible for the replacement, not the city." Big time gaveling and Our Mayor of Frownsville motioned the deputy to come get her. Frownsville was frantic. "Third," she was shouting now, "You have no legitimate reason to pass this special assessment except as a favor to your partners who will line your pockets with silver." She sat down just as the deputy arrived. "I'm done now," she whispered to him and smiled showing him she was no longer a danger to anyone.

The deputy looked at the Mayor who looked at the city manager who called for an end to the public forum. The Mayor hammered the gavel and you could almost see the corners of Mayor Gnome's mouth turn up as Walker put new batteries in his remote control.

CHAPTER 24
BLIZZARDS

Mrs. Miller cried and cried after the meeting. She thought she got us in trouble, and I think she was more worried about that than her own situation. We assured her we were okay. I mean, if they didn't haul Kristen out, what were they going to do to the rest of us? Kristen even stayed with us and had our agendas signed by Linda, so we could get extra credit in Social Studies. We were actually kind of giddy. I mean, we did it. We got the truth out. We just hoped someone listened.

Sean said some of the commissioners wrote stuff down when we talked, and Randy said that curly-haired guy down front was a reporter for the local paper so some of the truth was going to come out. We all felt a little bad about that because we wanted our paper to break the news first, but we had to do it for Mrs. Miller who still kept telling all of us to call her Doris. We hoped the paper didn't make a big deal of the Kristen thing, but she said if she could do it over again she'd walk right up front and grab that gavel from the mayor, bonk him on the cheap toupee, and finish off the city manager with an oak, nuts shot.

Everyone laughed, even Doris who won't let

Tommy swear. Kristen says a lot of things to get a re-action. I kind of wanted to say, "Soylent Green is Peo-ple" to Tommy and see if he'd do the fall on the side-walk thing in front of everyone, but I didn't. We all went to the Dairy Queen to celebrate our victory of sorts. Kevin paid for everyone, even Doris, and Tommy, and Mrs. Fortuni, but that was probably just to impress Kristen, who was still single. I had a caramel cashew Blizzard and a lot of Kristen's banana split. I figured I would do some push-ups at home, but I didn't.

We celebrated too soon.

Not only was Kristen not in the next day's paper, we were in it only as "scattered objections from govern-ment students." They played the whole thing up giving Walker's version of the facts almost word for word. "A fair, balanced solution designed to clean up unknown pollutants before they contaminate our drinking sup-ply." When Colbert read it, he said it was as fair and balanced as Fox News. Doris was given one line as a widower who might lose her house due to her husband's negligence. Man, does David Stevens write the news-paper too?

Mr. D. asked us what we would have done if we were the reporter on duty that night. Would we have written the rantings of a bunch of high school students or would we have played it safe and just printed what the city manager said. We were of course ready to print the truth as we saw it, but then we talked about libel. He asked if we had provided the council with documenta-tion and of course we had to say no, that we were never given the opportunity.

Sean finally nailed the solution. He suggested that a good reporter would have interviewed us afterwards to see what evidence we based our accusations on. Even if he didn't do that, the reporter could have given our names and said that we alleged the city manager is a lying thief or whatever. Good job Sean.

On Thursday, Knudson, the Government teacher, was questioned by Silvers about us disrupting the city's public forum. He told us that he told Silvers he knew nothing about it other than a number of kids turned in extra credit for attending a governmental meeting, and he assured Silvers that he would talk to all of his classes about appropriate behavior. Then Knudson wanted the inside information from us; what we were really doing disrupting a meeting. Kristen quickly told him that we just all needed extra credit because his tests were so hard. We all agreed, rather than tell him the truth about either the coming newspaper, or his tests.

This just made us more determined to get the paper out, quick.

CHAPTER 25
SIT DOWN, STAND UP, FIGHT, FIGHT, FIGHT

S o we began the edition. Some were giddy. Colbert loudly reminded us that the "truth will set us free." Sean kept printing out headlines and brought them to Anna for mock approval. TOTALLY EVIL CORPORATION SCREWS LITTLE OLD LADY WHILE CITY WATCHES. CORRUPT CITY MANAGER STEALS TAXES WHILE YOU SLEEP. WARREN RIEGLE GIVEN THE KEY TO THE CITY AND THE TREASURY. MAYOR WEARS A RUG, PICTURES ON PAGE FIVE. This was a lot of fun. LOCAL LITTLE LEAGUERS POISONED, LOSE NINE TO NOTHING. KSR CRAPS ON COMMUNITY; COMMUNITY CRAPS OUT. Alliteration. Thank you again Mrs. Neihardt. SHADYSIDE KILLER FOUND. THIRTY FIVE YEAR OLD CITY MANAGER RETIRES TO ARIZONA. BARRELS OF TOXIC WASTE POPPING UP EVERYWHERE; CITY RESPONSIBLE. MAYOR, CITY MANAGER AND CEO CAUGHT IN MENAGE A TROIS. SEAN ACES SAT, LSAT, ACT, AND THE SUNDAY CROSSWORD. And one more we couldn't use, COLBERT DECLARES PRESIDENTIAL BID; TRUMP STEPS ASIDE.

Anna did a heck of a job on this issue considering

the time constraints. We all did. We were determined to get the paper out and done right before the vote on the assessment. The people could rise up. Doris would be saved. My mom gave us fifty dollars for printing. My mom. Bryan's dad gave twenty. Oh and he quit KSR when he began to find out what was going on. Erin's dad got him a job in a small shop that made antique wheels for cars, and Bryan said he came home dirty and happy the first night. I think two other parents chipped in.

Once we did the big meeting, most of the parents knew something was going on. Sean said he'd have to be dead five days for his parents to look for the body. Middle of the night. The police come knocking on his parent's door. "There's been an accident Ma'am. I'm sorry to inform you that your son,..." "Son, I have a son? I remember being pregnant sixteen, no seventeen years ago." He'd do his voice real high. Other kids said their parents were asking a lot of questions. We took pictures of Shadyside, the power plant being built, KSR, Doris and Tommy and their house. Facts were questioned and re-questioned. Dombrowski hovered over every article checking every fact like a first-time mother. It got annoying.

Colbert wrote an editorial demanding the city back off the special assessment and let the DNR enforce the judge's order. This was what a newspaper was all about. You could feel it. Even the computers cooperated for a while. I thought Matt was going to have to write an article or take a picture. He looked lonely like he was waiting on a date who was late. And truthfully, I guess he was.

More truthfully, the paper was thin. It was KSR and filler, although Jake, always Jake on the sports page, did interview that baseball coach Silvers strongly suggested. Most of the stuff on him that we found interesting we couldn't put in the paper. Jake came back and said the guy must have been seven foot tall. Jake is tall, but he said Floyd, that was his name, could have easily rested his chin on Jake's head. Easily.

And it really wasn't a tryout with Toronto. It was a walk on circus, and they let him pitch five pitches. He said every pitch clocked over 95 miles an hour, but the catcher could only catch 2 of them. Toronto told him to come back when he got some control. Then Floyd made Jake catch for him. It scared him because it was so fast he didn't have the chance to even move his glove and he wasn't wearing a cup. Of course, when Jake told the story, he held his hand where the cup would have been and I tried not to look. Floyd said he still had it, and Jake could see that he did, but he only caught two of at least ten, and they hurt. It was much funnier when Jake told it, because he wound up and did all kinds of hand talking stuff. The stuff you can't put in the paper.

Nothing else in the paper is worth mentioning and the color sure wasn't in Floyd's story. Not to say the KSR, special assessment, etc., articles weren't well done. They had to be. The pictures were even pretty clear this time, but the headlines were pretty mediocre as I implied earlier. And that's how it went to print. We got a scare two days later. The printer called to say their press went down and I thought for sure "they" somehow got to our printer. But two days later the papers showed up.

We spent most of the hour proofing every page, which we had never done on a finished paper before. There was always a tangible level of excitement in the room before we distributed papers, but this one was different. The tingle was there, but there was the sense of a wake. It emanated from Dombrowski who was a lot more nervous than usual. Finally, when everything was judged accurate, we spread out to our assigned rooms. One paper per kid, one for the teacher, a stack for the library, a pile in the cafeteria, none for the office. This paper had an unwritten rule: If we had to keep it secret, the office wasn't going to like it. So no one dropped any off there.

I kept waiting for the boom. I mean, we were telling people they had been poisoned. If that didn't bother them, we told them they were being ripped off. After lunch, some of the teachers started questioning some of the students. About the third time I was asked, "Is this all true?" I wanted to say, "No, we made it up!" but I didn't. I just nodded yes. A few of them made comments about not trusting Walker or Riegle, and one said his mother lived out there, which I assumed meant Shadyside. Few students were riled. No mass implosion. Kristen and Erin seemed almost disappointed. We had done it, and no one cared, or at least cared enough to leave their classes, picket the city, and save Mrs. Fortuni and Mrs. Miller. We wanted more.

We got more the next day. Rumors were already spreading by the time we got to the Newspaper. There was a sub in place of Dombrowski, and he gave us nothing to do. Sit. Quiet. Okay, talk quietly if you must. Randy heard that Dombrowski was down in the office with Silvers, and a friend of his told him Silvers was furious, yelling and everything.

I told Kristen, "I saw my real estate agent in the parking lot this morning."

And she said, "It's probably true because I followed Walker and some other guy into the building. I almost slipped and fell from his slime trail."

Maggie heard that Dombrowski was fired and gone, but nobody wanted to believe that.

Erin told the sub she had to turn in a permission slip to the office, or she couldn't go on a field trip so the sub let her go. Subs always fall for that. She came back and said, "I could see Mr. D. in Silver's office with three other guys. The only one I knew for sure was Walker. No one was yelling."

The hour took forever. By third hour, Silvers had sent out his legions (secretaries and janitors) to collect all the papers. It seemed he didn't trust us to collect them.

They had barely begun when a television crew showed up to see the administration confiscate a second newspaper edition. I certainly didn't do it, but aren't cell phones great? The crew followed Silvers. He was interviewed right outside my third hour classroom and I could hear him telling the reporter that he was only trying to protect the school from libel suits. He had already been in contact with, and apologized to, community leaders who agreed, "A high school paper had no business impugning the reputations of these citizens. They were willing to graciously refrain from suing the school if the school did its best to collect the printed papers. That is why we are collecting them."

When the reporter asked to see one, Silvers said that would defeat the whole purpose. The administration didn't get many, but the TV crew did.

Sean hit the office at lunch time and there he sat, Mr. Dombrowski, in a room behind glass. He was like a little boy, everyone talking around him, but no one talking to him. Sean could see a few of our newspapers laid out on a table along with some other papers. Two of them were drinking coffee; Mr. Dombrowski had nothing. Sean left the office and went back to the cafeteria. He bought two pieces of pizza and a milk and went straight back to the office, ignoring Budd when she said he couldn't go in there, and he opened Silver's door and all those heads turned.

Sean just said, "I'm bringing Mr. Dombrowski his lunch."

"Thank you, Sean," was all Dombrowski said, but Sean said he smiled with his eyes.

Silvers said, "You need to leave."

Sean went back to the cafeteria where Colbert, Kristen and I were sitting and told us what he saw.

"Let's march right in there and demand they let him go back to his room and teach, because he was the best damn teacher in the building,"

Colbert got her to slow down. "We should get as many students together as we can and just sit in the office like they did in the sixties."

It was agreed. We grabbed Maggie, Randy, Erin and Bryan and they headed for the office. Kristen, Sean, Colbert and I stayed in the cafeteria recruiting others. We hit the newspaper kids first and then his English students, told them what was going on, and sent them straight to the office. Everyone went, and you might say that it was to get out of class, and for some it might have been, but for most, it was because they loved him the way you love a good teacher if you ever had one. By the time I got back to the office, there were probably thirty students, and Mrs. Budd was freaking. Colbert tried to get everyone to sit down quietly.

Silvers came out demanding what was going on from Budd. She said, "They won't leave. Make them leave."

Silvers told everyone to leave, and told Colbert to make them leave when Farroll, the superintendent, came out demanding to know what was going on. The two conferred with Budd, then they went back to Silvers' office to plot strategy. More kids tried cramming in but left the office doors open instead.

By the time the television crew returned (again, those cell phones), there were easily over one hundred kids spilling out of the office, into the hallway and back to the cafeteria. People parted for the anchorwoman, and this isn't important here, but she's not half as good looking in person as she is on television. She's skinny, but that's it. I heard someone yell, and I figured she stepped on his hand. Those cameras are actually kind of heavy. Why don't they use smaller ones? I could see kids videoing everything on their cells, which assured me it would hit YouTube before it hit the television.

Kristen and Colbert stood up. She spoke first to the camera. "We intend to stay here, on the floor, until they let Mr. Dombrowski go back to his classroom to teach."

"Why are they not letting him teach? Did he do something wrong?" the lady asked.

"No. He did everything right. He taught us to think. He taught us that when we see a wrong we need to right it. He taught us about the duties of a free press in a free society, and now they are trying to censor us for following those duties and doing the right thing."

"I saw the paper earlier. Are all those articles true?"

Colbert jumped in. "Mr. Dombrowski made us get two sources for every fact, which is not always easy. We have documents to back up everything we wrote, down in Dombrowski's room."

There was an announcement over the intercom from Silvers demanding all students and teachers to report to their rooms immediately, and attendance taken. Anyone not in the room will be given detentions.

Kristen said, "He's still not taking us seriously. We're not leaving."

Colbert said, "The people of this community deserve to know what is going on. Our industrial park and most of the surrounding neighborhoods are polluted with cancer causing chemicals. KSR is responsible for 96 to 97 percent of the chemicals and two years ago was ordered by a federal judge to begin clean-up immediately. They have basically ignored the order and hatched a plan limiting their costs to about 8 percent, and forced responsibility to the city for clean-up of any future discovered contaminations. The city is willing to take on this responsibility because they are partners with Warren Riegle, the CEO of KSR. The city manager, who is in that office right there," and he pointed at Silver's office, "right now with our principal and superintendent, is a secret partner in that same deal."

When he paused, Erin spoke up from the floor. "Don't forget Mrs. Miller, Mrs. Fortuni, and the others."

I was almost ready to jump up and speak but Kristen got it. "They are kicking Mrs. Miller and her son out of her house. Mrs. Fortuni's husband is already dead. We don't know if that is from this pollution, but there are a lot of people who are very sick and who have been drinking the pollution from KSR."

Right then Silvers and Farroll came out of the office. I think Silvers was all wound up to show Farroll how tough he was and that he still had control of the building so he was yelling, "Everyone out now!" They shoot dogs with less foam around their mouths. "You are all late for fourth hour and you will all be doing detention if it takes all summer." Farroll grabbed his arm and turned him directly to the camera. You should've seen the look on his face. It was on the nine o'clock news. It was on YouTube. He looked like he was punched in the balls and then forced to say, "Thank you sir. Could I have another." He did this fake smile thing and said, "No cameras."

The reporter asked, "Is Mr. Dombrowski being held in that office?"

Farroll pushed Silvers aside. "He is in there, but only because we are investigating his newspaper."

"Let him come out then," Kristen yelled.

"We haven't completed our investigation yet."

"What is to investigate? KSR polluted the water and became partners with the city and Walker to avoid paying to clean it up."

"You don't know that young lady."

"I do, and we have the evidence to back up everything."

"We are looking at the evidence now."

The anchorwoman asked, "Is Mr. Walker in the office, and would he care to come out for an interview?" Silvers left to check.

"You are going to need to leave. We need to get this school back to functioning as a school," Farroll said as if he were running for office. "We need these children back in the classrooms." It looked like he was trying to shoo her away, but he couldn't get within eight kids. Oh, and he did refer to us as children? Shows what he doesn't know about high schoolers.

Silvers came back and read a statement off a piece of paper. "Mr. Walker does not wish to be interviewed at this time. But he does say he doesn't know if Mr. Dombrowski has a personal vendetta against him or if he and the students had been duped by people within the community. Neither he nor the city are benefiting from the new power plant or the special assessment." If you think about that, it is true and clever. They hadn't benefited. Yet.

"Now, ma'am," Farroll said. "You will need to leave so that we can get these children back to their classrooms. They are playing for the camera." Farroll stood and waited for her to leave. The rest of us sat and murmured. The reporter got Colbert's and Kristen's name. Erin wanted us to sing "We Shall Overcome," which must have come from her Southern heritage. She started singing it softly and Bryan kind of hummed along but no one else joined in. It wasn't fair to compare us to the civil rights marches.

When the reporter was gone, Farroll faced us and told us, "You have five minutes to get to class. Anyone left will face suspension. If I need to call the police to clear this office, I will. Now go."

There was a stirring and everyone looked around, but no one moved.

Kristen spoke up. "Mr....I don't know your name. Are you new here?" I remember thinking, no, not him, Kristen.

"It's Mr. Farroll. I am the superintendent and I have been here seventeen years."

"That's nice. I've been here twelve years now. It's funny we've never met before."

"You are dangerously close to being insubordinate, young lady." He asked Silvers for her name.

"You don't need to ask him. My name is Kristen. I will write it down for you if you'd like. But that's not going to solve your problem. The police are never going to haul a hundred of us off to jail."

"We will begin calling parents."

"I'll give you my number and you'll have both me and my mom sitting on the floor."

"You have an answer for everything, don't you?"

"Chemistry gave me some problems last year, but I can get you out of this mess."

"Yes?"

"You can investigate everything in that paper all you want, and all you are ever going to find is the truth. If you find an error, which you won't, flunk us. Leave Mr. Dombrowski alone. It is our paper. He only taught us how to do it right. Announce to anyone who will listen that you are holding the papers so that you can double check the accuracy before releasing them again. When you finish, announce to the press how proud you are of all of us and give Mr. Dombrowski a raise, because I don't think that old car of his will make it through the summer. Give us back our teacher now; there are probably two or three students waiting for him in his classroom. It has to be just about time for fifth hour and I know I am dying to learn French since Ma and I are planning a trip to the Louvre this summer to get a close up on the Mona Lisa."

"Is this also something you learned from Mr. Dombrowski, or do you talk to everyone like this? It's all so simplistic to you and your cohorts," Farroll said with a sweeping gesture. "How are we to restore the good names of the people you libeled in your paper. There could be lawsuits. Mr. Dombrowski himself could be sued. This is supposed to be a high school, not the *Washington Post.*"

"It is not libelous if it is true. Why do you…." I suspect she was going to ask why he would take the word of a politician over that of the students he represented as a superintendent, but there was a disturbance outside the door. Students were clearing a path and a very angry Mr. Bennett came charging in demanding to know where Mr. Dombrowski was. I knew Mr. Bennett from Junior High, and he coached boy's soccer.

"Mr. Bennett, don't you have a class?" Farroll asked him.

"It is covered. You know you cannot question a teacher without union representation."

"We can if he doesn't ask for it."

"We both know he's too new to know his rights. I'm told he's been basically imprisoned here for five hours. Let me see him."

Farroll nodded him in, and more kids split apart to let him through. My butt was getting sore. Kristen tried to finish her questioning of Farroll but he ignored her. He whispered to Silvers.

Bennett came back out and demanded a private room where he could talk to Dombrowski, and Farroll told him to hang on. He turned to Kristen and said, "If we let him go, will you all go back to your classes?"

There was a lot of murmuring and Colbert said, "That's what we asked for."

"Okay. You may go back to your classes now. Mr. Bennett, he may come out."

Bennett came out first, followed by Dombrowski. Someone started a cheer and soon we were all yelling. It was kind of a standing ovation because we were all getting up anyway. Dombrowski grinned, but he looked embarrassed. There was no way out until we cleared the office, so he was stuck there. "They" were beaten.

CHAPTER 26
THE VOTE

Boy, were we screwed on that one. Sure, Farroll "released" him from the office, but he didn't let him go back to the classroom. Dombrowski was on something called administrative leave. That is where he is, suspended with pay pending an investigation, an investigation that of course was never going to happen. Purgatory.

I didn't find out until last hour, and Colbert and I went running down to the office. Mrs. Budd greeted us when we entered. "Well, if isn't the little commie hippy and his fat friend. They're all gone. If you want to sit back down on that floor, you go ahead."

She laughed. "You're not so smart now are you? In one hour, I'm going home too, to my nice warm house and comfortable bed. Why don't you and your commie friend just spend the whole night right there," she said pointing me to the floor.

I didn't know if she had been drinking or if she was always that filled with hatred. For a moment, I hoped she lived in Shadyside, but then I wouldn't wish that on anyone. I knew she still hated us a week later when we brought in a petition signed by all of the kids demanding the reinstatement of Dombrowski. She said, "Thank you reprobates," without moving her lips.

As we walked together down the hall, Colbert turned to me. "I may be a commie or a socialist or worse, a Goddamn Democrat or something, but you are not fat. Definitely not fat. Why does she have to be so hateful?" I thought he was going to reach for my hand which would have been okay. He didn't.

We entered sixth hour, tardy, which turned out to be my third one, detention. God how I hated high school at that moment. Then I remembered how Dombrowski used to tease us that the goal of any decent high school was to teach us to hate it. That way, when it was time for us to leave, we were ready to go. He said there was nothing more pathetic than someone stuck in high school still glorifying their days as a football star/cheer-leader. Life begins after high school. I tell you, I was ready for some life. Sixth hour took a long time, and I cried when I got home seeing Mr. Dombrowski's rust-ing car.

A strange thing happened in our community. There were some who were upset that Dombrowski was re-moved from the classroom, but they were mostly par-ents of the kids he had in class. And not even all of them were upset. There were some who were upset about KSR and their polluting the town, but the local newspa-per didn't play it up real big and the TV station only ran the story for one night, mostly about the sit-in and not why we did it.. No TV, no anger in America.

I think those who were upset mostly lived in the area around the industrial park. Colbert's source told him of one lady who stormed into the city offices demanding to know how the city could partner with a bunch of pol-luters, and she wanted the city manager fired and free city water. When she told them where she lived, they told her the pollution was basically on the other side of town. She thanked them and left. Colbert, when he was being Daryl, said he liked to think that being short sighted and greedy is a Republican attribute, but I'm beginning to think it is a people attribute.

Some were mad that school dollars were used to print the paper, and others were mad the paper was censored. Some teachers were upset it happened to Dombrowski, and some lived in fear it could happen to them. Some students cried at their loss, and others cheered they could have a sub and basically do nothing for the rest of the year. Everybody got something. Everybody except Mr. Dombrowski. Well, he got attacked. Someone in the city found a college picture of him protesting gay marriage. Apparently, he was for it. Where would they get that picture unless they had a lot of money to discredit him? He looked like a dork. That, they ran in the town's paper, not our articles. The letters to the editor pitied "us poor children" and questioned how such a man could ever have been hired.

What did I learn? Politicians only use sound bites because that's all the average American can comprehend, or at least their comprehension is limited to their attention span. We gave the community too much information at once and it wasn't information they wanted. People only say they are concerned. Schools only say they care about education.

Colbert's parents cared about him and spoke before the school board. School boards are a lot like city commissions. They only appear to listen, only pretend to care, and each member has their own private agenda.

If you get caught, attack the source and have a good public relations team available. Always threaten to sue. Be the good guy in the end and don't sue. Wait a week, smile, and people will forget everything. I was there.

If this sounds cynical, let me tell you what happened.

The first Tuesday in May, Kristen's birthday to be exact, the city council held its meeting in order to vote on the special assessment, the special windfall to KSR and Warren Riegle. City Manager Walker and Mayor Khronberg did their little song and dance for the audience recommending it as the best solution for a dire and unfortunate problem. Then they had to open it to community comment. That really meant us, because it was mostly us and a few people from Shadyside who came to talk of their illnesses. No one spoke for it. The mayor smiled at all of us and told us we each had two minutes to talk. He warned Kristen that she must behave herself, and she did. In fact, she choked up once and the mayor kept on smiling. I stood next to her at the mike but did not talk.

Doris cried and Mrs. Fortuni talked about her husband and called them all murderers if they let KSR off. There were two guys from the DNR who both said they weren't representing the DNR but representing themselves. They talked about how long it took them to shut down the pollution and get a court ordered cleanup, and how much more difficult it was going to be to do their job if the polluters expected to be let off the hook with a special assessment. They begged them not to pass it. As each person finished, the mayor smiled and said thank you. When he said, "Will there be anyone else?" and lifted his gavel, Mr. Dombrowski stood up. I hadn't even seen him enter.

"I have a few comments," he said. "My name is Bill Dombrowski." There was a stirring and murmuring amongst the commissioners. Dombrowski smiled. "I think a public forum is the best place for me to say that which I must say."

"Yes sir," and the mayor smiled while the television crew, which was not there for the last meeting, zoomed in. It was so quiet you could hear the little motor.

He talked very slowly and sometimes looked at notes, occasionally peeking up at the mayor. "I realize it is political suicide for me to speak before you tonight, but if I didn't, I would be a hypocrite. I try to live my life by example and these students have set an example for me by being here. I have tried hard to teach them," he gestured towards us, "that they must stand up when others are wronged, especially when it does not affect them. It seems they listened. I am new to teaching. This was my first job. Some might say that after two years of finding myself and five years of college, I messed up. I was notified today that my services will not be required next year."

Kristen said, "Those bastards," and I'll bet everyone heard but no one turned.

"After watching these students tonight, I realize I accomplished more than I ever could have hoped. This is most sad for me, not because I lost my job, but because I learned to love this community and these kids, and I am going to have to leave.

"I thank those in the community for supporting me, and I thank the community for entrusting their children to me. I tried to make a difference in their lives. The end result is unfortunate, but if I had to do it over again, I would do nothing differently. Nothing. I am so proud of these kids, these citizens, for uncovering a blatant evil within their community and then having the courage to do something about it.

"I like to look at the big picture. No that's a cliché and I passionately despise clichés. Let me tell you the future. I expect that you, the city commissioners, will pass this amendment tonight, and I expect you, Mr. Walker, will someday get rich off that power plant. I expect that these students now have the resolve to actually try to fight a corrupt system and improve this or any other community they chose to live in.

Maybe they even moved you just a little, gave you the birth of a conscience, or the thought that maybe next time you won't be able to get away with such crimes. I like to think that Mr. Walker, Mr. Riegle, and anyone else involved in the poisoning of the community will someday be punished, if not here, then by their maker." Lots of noise.

"May I ask a question?" "Yes, but you are running out of time."

"When is enough, enough?"

"I don't understand."

"Mr. Riegle is probably one of the wealthiest persons in the community, and I am sure Mr. Walker is paid very well for his services. You live in a beautiful community surrounded by wonderful people. What more do you need? Why do you have to be so greedy as to hurt people?"

"Mr. Dombrowski," Walker stood up. "I have agreed not to sue the school district for these libelous charges. But I have not agreed, not to sue you."

"Sir, I didn't come to argue, especially not on your home course. I need to accomplish two things for my own closure before I leave. I must apologize."

"Apology accepted."

"Not to you sir. To Mrs. Fortuni, to Mrs. Miller, to others who were ill or are ill. They deserve a public apology. Mrs. Fortuni, I am genuinely sorry for your loss. Mrs. Miller, I can only apologize to you because we could not do more.

"To the community as a whole. You trusted these people," he said pointing at the commissioners and Walker. "gave them a responsibility and are counting on them to do the right thing like these students did.

They are human beings and are weak. They failed you. I doubt very much they entered politics with the intention of participating in secret deals with the rich and powerful. I'm sure they intended to help their community and improve the lot of the people as a whole.

"Somehow the political system failed them, and then they failed the political system. I am hoping that just one commissioner has the courage to stand here tonight and say no to KSR. No to Mr. Walker. Yes to the community. Yes to the future of this community, these students."

There was a long pause, then he turned to us. "I guess that is what I had to say. Now I must say goodbye. I am so proud of you. You may lose this battle tonight, but you individually, are better for it. Remain vigilant. Make your communities better places to live, safer places to live. I am so proud of you." He was starting to choke up. "I guess I already said that." He turned and walked away from the mike. He said, "I will never forget any of you," as he walked out the door.

I ran after him and only learned the outcome later from Colbert. Dombrowski was the last to speak and Khronberg called for a vote. I think we all held out waiting for one to speak the truth and condemn the deal. The first three simply said, "Yay," as choreographed by Walker, but the fourth, Mary Lucas, stood up.

"You need to understand," she said to us. "There were partnerships and promises made long before your paper, long before even we found out. I don't really know if they are good things or bad things, but I know they are too far along to stop now. I admire your courage and wish I had as much. I promise you I will do all that I can for Mrs. Fortuni and Mrs. Miller. But I also must vote yay," she said turning to the mayor.

I knew we were sunk. No one else made a comment.

It was unanimous.

I'd like to say that Mary Lucas helped Mrs. Fortuni and Mrs. Miller, but she did nothing. In eighteen months, the city will begin procedures to steal the home of Tommy and Doris Miller. The power plant is getting bigger. Several people from Shadyside talked of suing everyone involved, but they don't have the money and law firms don't take cases that big on contingencies, especially when a city is involved.

Colbert's source said she had no solid evidence, but there were a lot of rumors going around the offices about what each of the commissioners got. One got a piece of land north of town at a bargain price. One got promises of future political support. One got a job at KSR for their son, and they all got trips to Florida on a company jet in order to stay at Warren Riegle's condominium on the ocean. It's a shame we no longer have a class, and a newspaper, and a backbone in which to report the real news

CHAPTER 27
THANK YOU'S

I caught Mr. Dombrowski in the parking lot. I didn't say a word. I could see that he too had been crying, but he was trying to hide it, you know, when a guy just kind of rubs his eyes a little with his sleeve, then his nose, then turns away. So, we walked, not really together but I was at his side and he knew I was there. I left my car at the city offices. Apparently we were walking home. It was only about four blocks so I would just have to leave early for school the next morning.

I tried to think of how to say that I was sorry, that I didn't want him to go. I wanted to say that I loved him and make him stop. You might think this was an inappropriate schoolgirl crush. Mr. Dombrowski would never love me because he loved us. Or even if it wasn't love, it was a level of caring that we could never get too much of. I think he knew when we published that paper he was done, but he did it. I think he probably saw the end back when we first met Mrs. Fortuni. It would have been easy for him to tell us that we couldn't investigate KSR or the city, because the school would not allow it, but he knew it was the right thing to do, and he was very big on doing the right thing. That was an act of love.

I hated the school. I hated the city. I hated KSR. I

wanted to say those things to Mr. Dombrowski too, but that was stupid. He never talked of hate, though he obviously had some anger in his little speech. He loved his books, his authors, the truth, us kids. That's the way I remember him best. We turned onto our road and neither of us had said a word. We walked much slower. He had long since stopped crying and was almost holding back a smile. How could he be happy?

When we got to Grandma's porch, he turned and stopped, and we finally looked at each other. He was fully smiling. How could what happened tonight make him happy? I didn't doubt that the commission voted for that stupid special assessment. Mrs. Fortuni? Mrs. Miller? And he was fired, the best teacher in the whole school.

"Lauren," he said. "Thank you for walking me home. It meant a lot to me."

"You're welcome, I guess."

"When are you going to pick up your car?" He smiled a little more.

"You noticed."

"It's not here."

"I'll leave early for school tomorrow. Mr. Dombrowski?"

"Yes."

"How can you not be angry after all that happened? You don't have a job. I'm sure they passed that assessment. The whole city's corrupt."

"Not the whole city, Hon. Did you see all the people who stood up tonight? All my students? You were there. You stood up."

"I didn't say anything."

"Last year would you have been there at all?"

"No."

"Are you going to make the world a better place, a

little less corrupt?"

"Maybe a little, but nothing like Colbert or Kristen."

"How could I not be happy?"

We said goodnight, but then he stopped and said, "Lauren."

"Yes."

"Do you know what this means?" I thought of love or at least some philosophical lesson. I shook my head no. "I don't have to decorate the gym for the prom." He laughed and it felt good to me. "Now if I could only get someone to go there with Matt. You?" I shook my head no, and he was still laughing when we went into our separate houses: mine my parents', his my Grandma's.

We had a serious May warm spell and it was beautiful. The grass greened out and the trees leafed in rebirth. I often saw Mr. Dombrowski sit outside and read or write in one of his journals. I never asked him what he was writing for. Students often came by after school, a lot at first, and then it tapered some. Kristen came once and they talked for at least an hour, and she didn't come see me.

Near the end of May I listened from my bedroom as he told my dad that he had just accepted a job in Michigan. He was going to teach on Beaver Island, a school for kids who deserved a second chance. I thought that was appropriate. He deserved one too. The kids there were lucky. He said he was expected there in two days. A teacher had gotten very ill and a friend recommended him. He offered to pay for June, but my parents wouldn't take it. I found the island on a map. It's way out in Lake Michigan. There's a campground there.

I knew when he was leaving. I watched him load his car. He really didn't have much stuff, but the back end looked like it was riding low and I wondered how that thing would get to an island way up there. I thought of calling Kristen so she could call all the other kids and we could say goodbye and that we loved him and would miss him, but I didn't. I just watched from my window. He rang our doorbell, but mom and dad weren't home, so he left the keys inside the screen. He checked the oil, closed the hood and started it up. He was going to need a muffler. He began to back up. Then he stopped, right in front of my window. He got out, looked right at me and said goodbye. I just mouthed the words, "Thank you."

End

ABOUT THE AUTHOR

Bruce Loper is happily married with two wonderful kids. There. That is out of the way and while it sounds common, these are the most important things. Though retired, he keeps busy writing, skiing, golfing, camping, living. Michigan is without a doubt the best state in the union. He did thirty years in high school classrooms and six years teaching college. It almost sounds like it took him thirty years to graduate high school. Somewhat less than that. He loved every single minute in his classrooms and I think every student who passed through his door. He is currently three books deep on a humorous detective series and is thrilled when he gets feedback from people who identify with, hate, or love his characters. He also makes artistic fish which satisfy a darkly disturbed creative need and several galleries have generously donated space for said fish. On his tombstone it should read,

"HE REALLY TRIED
TO MAKE THE WORLD
A BETTER PLACE THAN HE FOUND IT."